# GORY DAYS
## ROCK & ROLL NIGHTMARES '80s EDITION

### SHORT STORIES

### EDITED BY

### STACI LAYNE WILSON

Copyright © 2021 by Staci Layne Wilson

Published by Excessive Nuance in paperback
ISBN-13: 978-0-9675185-8-9

Also available via e-book & audio

# OTHER
## ROCK & ROLL NIGHTMARES

ALONG COMES SCARY ('60s EDITION)

DO YOU FEAR LIKE WE DO ('70s EDITION)

**COMING SOON**

NONFICTION EDITION

MOVIE EDITION

# CONTENTS
## GORY DAYS

## Don't Stand So Close to Meat
Staci Layne Wilson

*Monday Menu*
Roast Duckling with Merlot-Chocolate
Sauce and Roasted Beets
with Merlot and three drops of blood

They only think they love you. Granted, they love your music. They love the way you look, the way you move. But they don't love *you*. Not like I do.

How can I get you to love me back? I know you love my food. That's why you hired me to be your personal chef in the first place. But the emphasis has remained on *chef*, not personal. How many times have we had an actual conversation? Ten, maybe 20? Would it surprise you to know that I can recount all of them?

Our very first conversation was when you wooed me away from Chez Laverne. You walked into the kitchen to compliment my pâté en croûte with inlay, and I was over the moon. You understood that the bread needs to be brown and crisp, the forcemeat must be fully cooked, and the inlay of meat down the middle cannot, under any circumstances, be overdone. You loved the flavorful gelée topping, comparing it to heaven. It took me 24 hours to create that dish, but when it was ordered, I did not know who it would be for. When Chef Dubois told me it would be on the menu as a special order, I was surprised but not overly so. As you know, Chez Laverne is quite exclusive and a favorite celebrity hangout. But I hadn't seen you there before that night. Not in the flesh, anyway.

I knew who you were, of course. It's impossible to be alive in 1984 and not have heard your album *Food of the Gods*. It's gone triple-platinum, hasn't it? The culinary twist on your songs, your love of fine cuisine, is certainly a hit amongst young junior and sous chefs like myself. It's impossible to work in a kitchen without hearing Otto Larsen blasting from someone's boom-box at least a few times a week.

But not until I looked into those dark blue eyes of yours—so earnest, so direct—did I *really* know who you were. You're a man of wealth, talent, and style. But you are missing out. Sure, those groupies give you what you want, but only I can give you what you need. *If I can get you to notice me.*

I have one week before you are set to leave on tour. I want to go with you. Not as your cook, but as your woman.

For the ancient Greeks, blood was a magical elixir. Pliny the Elder wrote of the mad rush of spectators into arenas to drink the spilled blood of fallen gladiators in hopes that they, too, would become strong and fearless. If you consume my blood, will you absorb something of me? Let's find out.

Your dinner is there on its silver platter. Your glass of Syrah sits breathing... *bleeding*. I have given you three drops. *You've shown remarkable restraint, Grace.*

Right on time comes your butler, James. He gives me a curt smile, then goes to the tray. He picks it up with a practiced, expert sweep of his hand, and then heads off into the dining room. To you.

I follow, ready to recite the ingredients of tonight's meal. I know you'll be tired. And ravenous. I heard you rehearsing your new setlist while I prepped and cooked all this afternoon. It's hard to pick just one, but I think my favorite song is *Insatiable*. The title has something to do with it for sure, and the lyrics are appropriately saucy, but it's the guitar break that gets me going. I imagine your hands on me, playing me like your instrument.

James and I enter the dining room, and there you are, reading *Rolling Stone*. Not *CREEM*. Certainly not *Hit Parader*. You have more class than that. You look up from the article and move the magazine aside.

Your eyes seem black in the soft, dim candlelight, but I catch the glints of blue. The music journalists compare you to Klaus Meine. Lazy. Just because you are of Germanic heritage, wear leather onstage, and have long black curly hair. You are so much more than he will ever be—you are a genius. A legend.

"I'm famished!" you say with your devil-may-care grin.

I knew you would be, Otto.

James sets the entrée down, and then—thank God—exits the room.

You're admiring the dish before digging into it. You don't like appetizers or salads, so I don't serve them. You go right for the meat. The wine. And, sometimes, dessert. But not for the past few weeks. You're getting in shape for the tour. You told me, and I listened.

"Looks delicious," you say. I catch a whiff of your cologne. Dior Fahrenheit. Popular, but you make it your own. There's the aggressive leather top note, followed by lavender, mandarin orange, hawthorn, nutmeg, cedar, bergamot, chamomile, and lemon. It's your own musk that brings it to life.

"Delicious," I repeat dreamily.

You're taking a hearty bite. You didn't notice what I'd said. As usual.

I give you a brief rundown of the ingredients, then I say, "It's the wine pairing that really makes it sing, though. You will notice black cherry, supple tannins, and a chocolatey finish." And blood, blood, blood. *Drink it.*

You take an obligatory sip, the red of my blood meeting your curved lips. Will you notice the Band-Aid on my left pinky finger, Otto?

You set the wineglass aside. "Thank you, Grace. That'll be all."

Dismissed.

Tomorrow, I will be bolder.

*Tuesday Menu*
Pork Loin with Cider-Madeira Sauce and earlobe
with Pinot Blanc

Poultry shears have more than one use. Mine are kept razor-sharp, but just to be sure the procedure is as quick and painless as possible, I oil my stone and run the blades across it a few times. The steel gleams in the flow of the water as I rinse the scissors in your sink. *Our* sink… soon.

For now, I feel blessed to have a true chef's kitchen just to work in. Your entire home is a showplace, of course—I love how one can see the whole Valley below and Downtown Los Angeles beyond from this vantage point—but this room is the heart and soul of it all. It's where your nourishment comes from. *You have devoured my soul, why not my body too?*

The sauce is nearly done. It burbles in the stainless-steel pot on the black porcelain range with its 8,000-Btu gas burner set to simmer. James will be here in about ten minutes, so it's now or never.

I sweep my long brown hair over my left shoulder, then pin it up and out of the way with a metal duckbill clip. Pinching my lobe between my thumb and forefinger, I pull it tight, and, using the shears in my right hand, *SNIP!*

No hesitation. I just did it. *Hey, Grace, you're pretty dang sharp.* No pun left behind! It doesn't even hurt. I grab the waiting bandage, and then wrap my ear quickly and tightly before it can leak. Easy.

As I cross the Spanish-tiled floor to the cutting board where the shallots are waiting to be minced, I suddenly feel woozy. I drop my earlobe onto the counter, then use the marble edge to steady myself. *Deep breaths, Grace.* In through the nose, out the mouth. Okay. I feel steady now.

I must work quickly. I put the earlobe next to the shallots and use my paring knife to chop everything into minuscule bits. I add the mixture to the sauce and stir. The smell of onion and flesh is quickly consumed and obliterated by the tang of cider and fortified wine.

When you taste this, Otto, you won't notice anything is amiss. But if I'm doing this right, you will *know*. Your soul will know it has found its mate.

I touch the bandage covering my severed ear. It's a bit sore. I look on the bright side, thinking that a lost earring won't be such a tragedy anymore—I'll always have a backup.

James is here. He barely looks at me, he just takes your food and goes. I remove the clip from my hair and smooth it down before following the butler into the dining room.

You're wearing jeans and you haven't buttoned your shirt all the way up. I can see the hollow of your throat and a hint of each clavicle. God, you're beautiful.

Do you think I'm beautiful too? You haven't said as much, but you're a gentleman. Not like those misogynistic barbarians from Motley Crüe or Twisted Sister. Hair bands… heathens! I'd heard all about their exploits from my colleagues on the Sunset Strip. Not that we'd ever catered to such riff-raff at Chez Laverne. They were more suited to pizza and Long Island iced teas at The Rainbow Bar & Grill.

You prefer fine dining. That's how I know you are special, Otto. You have taste. Now… *taste me.*

"Tonight, you have tender pork loin drizzled with cider-madeira sauce and paired with a 1972 pinot blanc that is sweet and slightly acidic. Bon appetite." I smile.

I watch as you shear off a small slab of the meat with your knife, fork it into your mouth, and chew. Your eyes glaze with obvious pleasure. "Mmm," you sigh sensuously. "I'm sure going to miss you while I'm on tour."

*You will? Really? Why not take me with you? I could make you so happy, Otto.* "I can only imagine what's to eat backstage."

You grin, take another bite of my one-of-a-kind creation, then nod. "It's pretty grim. Sweating bologna, dried American cheese, and—" you grimace – "white bread."

Perish the thought! "But surely a musician of your stature rates better than that?"

You shrug. Self-deprecating. I love that about you. You don't flaunt your fame. Yes, your home is grand with its million-dollar view and state-of-the-art recording studio, gold and platinum records lining the hall walls. But some artists need the finer things in life to keep the muse piqued. You take another bite.

I'm feeling a little awkward standing here, but you haven't dismissed me, so that must mean you want me to stay. Oh, how I'd love to join you in a meal. I flick my hair over my shoulder. Will you see the bandage and ask me what happened? Will you care that I'm hurt?

"Thank you," you say. "See you tomorrow."

I get it. A mere ear wasn't enough. Lopping a lobe was a grand gesture in Van Gogh's day, but the 1880s and the 1980s are worlds apart. I have to be brash, bold, loud, and lavish. It's got to hurt.

*Wednesday Menu*
Chicken Satay Burger, Lyonnaise
Potatoes, and Small Toe
with Australian Chardonnay

Back in your kitchen. Soon to be *our* kitchen. Will we have our own private chef, or shall I continue to feed you? They do say that the best way to a man's heart is through his stomach. And I enjoy planning menus for you—anticipating what you desire gives me such pleasure.

As I feed the plump, organic chicken breasts through the meat grinder, I add my small toe. Don't worry, I washed it, and it's been on ice ever since I left my apartment this afternoon.

I read somewhere that the severing of a small toe is an initiation requirement for the Hell's Angels Motorcycle Club. It is enough to count, but not enough to affect the balance because it's the big toes that bear the brunt of our weight when we walk. I do feel a little off, but I'll get used to it.

I cauterized the stump with my crème brûlée torch so there's no blood, but it does throb. I'm wearing sandals to allow the wound the air it needs. Will you notice? Will you ask what happened? I won't bring it up, because I want to see if you will.

The toe has blended seamlessly into the chicken. Now I'll form the patty, broil it, and toast the brioche bun. I can smell the potatoes in the oven, and I can tell everything will come together perfectly for your 6 p.m. dinnertime. You are so punctual. I've read that most rock musicians are chronically late, dismissive of others' time, unreliable. Not you, Otto. Yet another quality that sets you apart from your brethren.

While I wait for everything to bake and broil, I flip through the *Rolling Stone* you were reading the other night. Your tour dates are in it, along with an incredibly sexy, full-page color photograph of you. God, your eyes are so deep, so wise. Your body, drug-free and fueled by only the best ingredients, is lean and taut. You sit in your recording studio with your legs spread and your jeans overly tight, you naughty man. I can't wait to show you how naughty I can be, too. Every city on the tour will hold a new, exciting hotel room adventure for us.

It's time to assemble your meal and bring it to you. I'll limp—just a little—and you'll ask me what's wrong. I'll laugh and say, "Oh, it's nothing! I'm fine." You'll offer to kiss it and make it better, and then… then…

James is here. He barely acknowledges me. We will fire him, Otto. He's got bad energy. He doesn't respect you, either. Did you notice how he slammed your dinner plate down last night? It clattered, and he didn't even apologize to you. He takes the platter and leaves the kitchen. As usual, I follow. I think I should be the first one out; after all, I am the chef, and he's a glorified waiter.

You look tired. You've been rehearsing for hours, perfecting your set. The band left as I was arriving. Brett looked at me and smiled, but Günter just ignored me as he strode past, clutching his bottle of Jack Daniels as if his life depended on it. I honestly don't know why you put up with them. You deserve better.

James sweeps by me, brushing past with such rudeness that I teeter. My amputation zings as I regain my footing. You're not looking. I inch closer, my sandaled toes peeking from beneath the crisp crease of my black slacks. Still, nothing. *Damn.*

"Ahhh," I wince.

You look up at me. Now I've got you.

"Are you okay?"

"Oh, yeah," I shrug and smile. "Just hurt my foot."

You turn your attention back to your dinner. "Chicken or turkey?" you ask.

I limp closer. I wobble, then put my hand on your shoulder to steady myself. Oh, my God. Your skin feels so warm through the thin material of your shirt. Your muscles are rock-hard. You don't seem to mind that I'm touching you... Do you like it?

"Steady, there," you chuckle, then... Oh, hell no. You moved my hand off your shoulder? What the fuck?

I feel the blood rush to my cheeks. How embarrassing. I have to do something. Say something. Oh, God. "Um, sorry." *Idiot.* (Me, not you, of course. You were just taken by surprise, is all.) "It's, uh, chicken."

"Cool," you mutter. You're staring at your plate. Is there something wrong? My presentation is gorgeous. There cannot be anything wrong. You look up at me. I've put some curls in my hair for this evening—will you say I look pretty? "There will be a guest for dinner tomorrow."

Oh. "Any dietary restrictions?"

You shrug. "I don't think so."

"Okay. I'd planned on Mussels Provencal with this amazing Chilean sauvignon blanc I picked up at the wine market in Santa Monica."

"Sure." You bite into your burger. I've been dismissed.

Driving home. Good God, it hurts to press the gas and brake. Why didn't I think to cut off the left toe instead of the right? But pain is temporary—my love for you is forever. I'm not really thinking about that particular hurt, anyway. What I want to know is, who are you having for dinner tomorrow? Me, of course... but you don't know that. Is it Brett and Günter? No, you indicated it was only one person. A woman? No, you don't have a girlfriend. Maybe it's Sid... your manager clearly doesn't like me, so I sure hope it's not him.

*Thursday Menu:*
Mussels Provencal, muscle strips
with Chilean Sauvignon Blanc
(for two)

I can hardly believe my eyes. There you are, sitting next to a sleazy slut. And you're all over her! She's not your type—what are you thinking? James serves you both, and I am speechless. I can't stay.

Back in the kitchen. My sanctuary. I'm trembling. I can hear you two giggling. *Giggling!* You! This is beneath you, Otto. Sure, a man has needs, I know... but bringing such trash into our home? Unacceptable.

I feel sick. My stomach is churning. I want to puke. But I can't take the risk right now. It'll strain my upper trapezius. I sliced out only a thin strip, but I must be careful for a few days, at least. *Ugh!* I can't even put my hands around her stupid neck to strangle her. Might be worth it, though. Oh, Otto. How could you?

More laughter. She'd better not be laughing at me. Whores like her always think they're better than me. Because I'm not blonde. Not stacked. Not skinny. Not cool. *But I'm better than you will ever be, bitch. Otto just needs to see me, really see me, and then he'll dump your ass. What the hell are you laughing about?*

I inch my way back to the dining room from the kitchen. I stand in the shadows, listening. I don't hear silverware clinking. You're not eating? What are you doing? Holding my breath, I peer around the corner.

*No.*

Your hand is on her braless breast. "You've got great tits," you say, nuzzling her ear. She's got her hand on a part of you that's meant for me. This is so wrong. So, so wrong. "Come on tour with me, baby."

*What?! That is it!*

A terse whisper in my ear: "Grace, what are you doing?" It's James. The nosy bastard.

But I can't let him see my anger. I muster a shaky smile. "Oh, um… just wanted to see if Otto needs anything else before I go." Another smile. Better this time.

He levels me in a steely, unmoved glare. "You may go."

But I'm not going anywhere. I drive off the property, and then park my car down the block. I limp back to the house, waiting, concealed until I see James leave. I let myself back in through the kitchen door. The house is dark. Quiet.

I hold my breath, listening intently. No... not entirely quiet. I hear your music, Otto. Are you seducing her with your own songs? Kind of tacky. But I can't blame you. What better aphrodisiac?

I hate her. Just as the thought enters my mind, my eyes flick to the Maplewood knife block. I saunter over to it. It would be so easy. My fingertips play on the handle of the carving knife. No. I'll need the cleaver. I slip it from its sheath and hold it up. I see my face reflected in the blade. *Nice knife, Grace. It really brings out the murder in your eyes.*

My mind flits to Sweeny Todd, the Demon Barber of Fleet Street. But I have no partner in crime, no Mrs. Lovett. It's just me. I need to think. I could serve her to you—serve you right. How should she be dished up? Quiche Lorraine, Steak Diane, Sloppy Joanna? First, I have to get her alone. I hold the cleaver close to my heart, and I wait.

Endless hours later, nearly dawn. Almost light, but she doesn't notice me driving behind her. Stupid girl.

*Friday Menu*
Breast Pâté
with Brut Rosé Champagne
and a surprise pudding

I wanted to surprise you with tonight's dish, Otto. But I'm the one who's surprised. James just fired me. I know you didn't want to hurt my feelings, but you have. Why couldn't you talk to me about this? James says my behavior is inappropriate. He says you're not comfortable having me in your home anymore. He even used the words "fanatical" and "obsessed."

"You misrepresented yourself," James is saying when I drive the boning knife into his eye. His hands come up, tremble in midair, and then he crumples to the ground without a sound.

*As cold in death, as in life.*

I must act fast. I take James by both of his arms and drag him into the pantry. I then shut the door. Now what? I will see my pre-firing plan through. I have to make you understand. I will make you love me, even if it kills me.

A lightning bolt of agony in my chest. I ignore it. *Act.*

I turn around to face the counter. The meat is on ice. I planned to make pâté, but there is no time now. Tartare it is, then. I carefully remove the two mounds from the ice, then set each gelatinous mass on its own plate. One cut is clearly superior—we'll see, Otto. You'll see. And you'll understand.

Where are you? It's not time for dinner yet, but I check the dining room anyway. No. The recording studio? Are you alone? You must be—I didn't see your bandmates' cars in the drive. I need you to be alone for this. Intimacy calls for privacy.

I descend the stairs to your basement studio, praying that I won't fall. But God won't let me fall. This is too important. But oh, how I hurt. Each damaged body part screams in wrath—my ear, my toe, my upper shoulder. And of course, the freshest wound is the loudest. I feel dizzy. *No. Ignore it. Be strong, Grace. For Otto.*

There you are. I see you through the small window in the door. The red light centered above is on, indicating that you're recording. I don't care. This is more important.

The platter is getting heavy. Using my upper back to push the door open, I enter the room. *Ta-da!*

You don't turn around. You keep your back to me. What the hell? Oh, I see. You're wearing your headphones. I lay the food down on the low coffee table in front of the pot-reeking sofa. I approach you. No response. How can you not know I'm here? You should smell my perfume. You should feel the radiance of my love. Have I been wrong about you all along? No. You just haven't seen the light yet.

I'm right behind you now. God, I want to stroke your beautiful black hair, feel the strands tease my fingers. But there will soon be all the time in the world to make love with you. I tap your shoulder.

You're startled. You don't smile, but I can see something in your eyes. Fear. You're afraid of me, Otto? Why? All I've ever done is feed you, love you.

You stand, removing your headphones. "Grace," you say. You look into my eyes, and then you glance down and notice that I am bleeding. Hard to hide in this white chef's coat, but if things go well, I won't be wearing it much longer. *Wink.*

I smile. "Yes, it's me. I've brought your dinner."

"Um." Your Adam's apple bobs. "Did James, uh, talk to you?"

I shrug, playing dumb. You like dumb girls. Last night proved that.

"Well, Grace, this is never easy, but..."

"Dinner is served," I announce, cutting you off. A bit rude, I know, but you won't want to say what you were about to, once you see what I've brought you.

You seem nervous. Your eyes follow the direction of my pointing hand.

You gasp, then cry out. I don't blame you. My breast is beautiful. Better than hers, which sits wilting in the plate next to mine. You've finally seen the light, haven't you, Otto?

*Inmate # E-94607*
Breakfast: Scrambled eggs
Lunch: Fish sandwich
Dinner: Hamburger helper

More like scrambled dregs, shit sandwiches, and hamburger help-me. Being stuck here in this "jack in the box" behind bars is even worse than Death Row. Why, oh, why did California abolish capital punishment? This is adding insult to injury. Yeah, I'm being a bit dramatic. I'm glad there's no Death Row. I do want to die, but not just yet. I have one plan to carry out before I go.

And at least I have groupies. What do you think of that, Otto? Bet you're jealous. I get all kinds of letters, all kinds of pleas. They want me to cook for them. They want *me*.

There is someone special. His name is Colton, and he writes to me every day. He's my Lovett, my partner in crime. We are working on a cookbook together. He wants to call it *Killer Recipes*, but I think that's a little on-the-nose. He says we'll sell a million copies, which will help pay for the appeal. We need a top-notch attorney. I can't believe you shared that recording with the cops, Otto.

That was a low blow. But once I get out, I can explain everything to you. Why wouldn't you let me explain?

The cookbook will have the most amazing recipes of famous rock stars' meals. Everything from Mama Cass's lowly ham sandwich to Rick "Strummer" Rozetti's ortolan delicacy.

If only I could cook you like an ortolan, Otto. Do you know the process? It's quite delicate... and depraved. The small songbirds are force-fed figs, and then drowned and marinated simultaneously in a cauldron of the finest French Armagnac. The sodden fowl are then roasted, plucked, and eaten whole from feet to beak. *Crunch.* I've ever eaten them, myself. But I've read that the flavors of fruit, brandy, dark flesh—and your own blood as your tongue is pricked by sharp bones and claws—are second to none. Like you. You deserve nothing less, my love, than to be my last meal.

*Ugh.* If only I could say prison food is anywhere near as mouthwatering as the thought of roasted Otto-Ortolan. This slop tastes like Betty Crocker and Charles Manson had a tawdry affair. I push the mush with my plastic spork. All the inmates around me are eating heartily. How *can* they?

Colton says I need to keep my strength up for my appeals. He's right. What to eat? Everything is beige. The chicken, I suppose.

I bring the drumstick to my mouth. It smells like rancid grease and feels like a barely-warm sponge. I close my eyes and bite in. I can't stand to have it in my mouth for more than a second.

*Just get it down, Grace.* I swallow. Gulp.

A bone catches, only this isn't from some small songbird. I'm in trouble!

Can't swallow. Can't breathe. Can't see...

## Sharp-Dressed Manslaughter
Sean McDonough

**1987**

Brett knew what was happening the moment the car's stereo started squealing like a tortured pig.

"No!" he screamed out loud. He scrambled for the eject button and fumbled to pull the cassette tape free, hoping against hope that it was intact and then wailing in utter despair as a tangled mess of magnetic tape came pouring out of the cassette deck like disemboweled intestines.

"Fuck!" Brett screamed. He slammed his fist against the dashboard, furious with the car but angrier with himself. He knew full well that the old Trans Am's cassette player was a serial tape slaughterer. If he could have just waited another half-hour to play the cassette...

Brett cradled the butchered remains of the latest Manslaughter album. Half of the tape was still tangled in the jaws of the car's stereo, but maybe if he was careful—

A horn blared in his ears. Brett dropped the tape and jerked the Trans Am back into his own lane, narrowly avoiding the chugging Cadillac coming up in his blindspot. He cranked down his window just far enough to stick his middle finger out as the other car before pulling over to the side of Sunset Boulevard.

The cassette tape had fallen into the footwell of the passenger seat. The unspooled tangle of tape gaped back at him, twisted into an agonized wail that mirrored his own distress.

Brett's blood pounded in his ears. The longer the teenager looked at the ruined Manslaughter album, the louder the sound in his head became. The rushing blood drowned out the traffic roaring past him. It blotted out the voice of his mother telling him that he took things too seriously. It washed away the mantra that Doctor Viola had told him to repeat whenever he felt like he was about to lose his temper:

*I breathe out hot. I breathe in cool.*
*I breathe out hot. I breathe in cool.*
*I breathe out hot. I breathe in cool.*
*I breathe—*

He reared back and slammed a motorcycle boot into the dashboard. "Cocksucking! Fucking! Useless! Piece! Of! Shit!" Brett kept going, punctuating every word with another kick. The volume knob broke off. The preset buttons snapped under his heel and clattered to the floor like broken teeth.

He could have gone on forever. He barely felt the entire car chassis rock with every blow. He didn't even hear the sound of groaning metal from inside the engine. It wasn't until Brett saw the smoke rising from under the hood that he came back to his senses. He flung open the door, heedless of a city bus that nearly turned him into paste, and scrambled around to the front of the car. The old Trans Am was smoking like the floor of Gazzarri's on a Saturday night. Brett popped the hood and was rewarded with a belch of heat and the stench of burning rubber.

The car was totally shot. Brett could tell that much with a single look. He dropped his hands to his side. The hood slammed back down a second after, as final and authoritative as a coffin lid slamming shut.

The sound was a reminder that Brett didn't need. He knew what the closing hood meant.

No car meant he couldn't get to work. And if he couldn't get to work, he couldn't keep stuffing money in the coffee can under his mattress. If he couldn't save money, he couldn't afford to move out after graduation. That meant no moving to L.A., no chance at getting a job at the Rainbow, and a guarantee that he would spend the rest of his life stocking comic books and living in his mother's back room!

*If I ever make it home,* the teen realized. No way the steaming wreck in front of him was getting back to Hidden Hills. He didn't even have a quarter for a payphone. Brett scanned the oncoming traffic. He knew exactly what he looked like—six wiry feet of juvenile delinquent, six and a half if you counted the blown out mass of blonde hair. Not the kind of hitchhiker a church van would pick up, but he held out hope for a GMC van or another Trans Am. A couple brothers in metal... or maybe some sisters. That wouldn't suck.

"Rough day, brother?"

Brett spun around. He had been too distracted to notice where he'd pulled over. Most of the stores along this stretch of cracked concrete were typical chain shit. But directly in front of him, sandwiched between a Radioshack and a Supercuts, was a cramped store with a smudged window surrounded by faded wood paneling.

The person who'd called out to him leaned in the doorway. The guy looked to be about 50, but the bushy beard and gravy-stained tie dye t-shirt said that he'd missed the starting gun for the rat race and was in no hurry to catch up.

"Car troubles?" he asked, and Brett could only shrug. It seemed self-explanatory.

The big hippie waved in toward his shop. "Come on in. I've got a phone. Let's see if we can get you where you need to go."

He went back inside without waiting to see if Brett followed. The teenager hesitated for a moment, but what else was he going to do? He stepped onto the sidewalk, stopping only briefly to look at the sign over the door before going inside:

*Just Right Goods.*

Brett stepped inside, and his first thought was that never before was there a store with a more misleading name. Mismatched antiques and weird shit crowded on every surface. Calling it a thrift shop was too mundane. This wasn't just whatever Aunt Gladys had in her closet when she died. This was decades of bizarre shit from every corner of the planet. Brett saw dust-covered black and white photos crowded next to a ship in a bottle. He narrowly avoided jabbing his thigh with a fucking Three Musketeers sword haphazardly poking out of an umbrella stand.

"By the way, I dig the patches, man," the shopkeeper called out from behind a moth-eaten curtain.

"Thanks." Brett didn't need to look down. He knew the insignias decorating his denim jacket by heart. Alice Cooper. Dokken. Skid Row. Most prominently, the massive

Manslaughter logo emblazoned across his back.

The shopkeep emerged with an old rotary phone in hand. The phone line dangled behind him and barely stretched far enough to rest atop the glass counter next to the register. "Did you get the new album? What's it called, *Got a Reason*?"

"*Gimme a Reason*," Brett corrected automatically. "Yeah, I came down from Hidden Hills to pick it up."

"They don't have record stores in Hidden Hills?"

"They've got malls," Brett said scornfully.

The burly storekeeper laughed. "I get that. Those places got everything except a soul, am I right?" He nudged the phone a little closer. "Anyway. All yours, man."

Brett dialed, and knew by the third ring that his mom wasn't going to pick up. Today was bridge day. Or maybe tennis. He hung up before the answering machine even came on. In the silence that followed, he shrugged awkwardly at the old hippie behind the counter.

"Well, thanks anyway," Brett said. He turned back toward the door, wondering if he could maybe scrounge enough coins for bus fare from under the seats.

"Kid, hang on," the shopkeeper called.

Brett swung back around. The old man was surveying him carefully. Beetle-black eyes peered at him from within a deep nest of wiry salt and pepper hair.

"You really drove all the way to Hollywood for a cassette tape? Tell me why. No bullshit this time."

Brett hesitated. He would have told him the truth—this weird old bastard would probably get it better than anyone—but he stumbled over how to explain why he felt the need to drive all this way. The words eluded him, the same way they always did.

To drive down to Hollywood for a record made him feel the same way he felt at a show. Any show, really, but most of all a Manslaughter show. What Brett didn't know how to say was that the best music was *earned*. And if you did earn it, Christ, it made your bones hum just right. Fuck 40 minutes of traffic with busted A/C, Brett would crawl through broken glass for just a whiff of that feeling.

Brett still did not have those words. He had nothing but another shrug. "It just feels right," was what he said.

The shopkeeper grinned, baring a mouth of yellow teeth. "Feels right... I like that." He rummaged underneath the counter. "For me, that was Joe Creeps in 1965," he called out with his head down, out of sight. "Just a guy from Arizona with an acoustic guitar, but damned if he didn't make a just-drafted, 19-year-old kid from New Jersey feel like there was a place in the universe where he belonged. I hitchhiked all the way to Arizona to see him live… it just felt right."

The older man emerged back up from under the counter. "I got something for you. One kindred spirit to another…" He tossed a white bundle in Brett's direction. The teen caught it on reflex and let it unfold in his hands.

It was a t-shirt. The cotton felt like gauze in his hands after too many runs through the wash, and it smelled vaguely damp, but Brett couldn't care less. He gaped in slack-jawed wonder at the image emblazoned across the front of the shirt—a cadaver underneath a sheet in a morgue. One foot protruded from under the sheet with a tag dangling from the toe.

"This is from the D.O.A. tour," Brett gasped.

The shopkeeper nodded. "'82. Manslaughter's last regional tour before they hit the big time. Just a couple states out East."

"New York, New Jersey, D.C.," Brett recited. The old hippie nodded along. "Right. Good luck finding one of those anymore, but I'd say you could give it a home."

The empty void in Brett's wallet had never felt like more of a black hole. "I don't have any cash, but if you could hold it for a week—"

"It's yours, kid. Seems to me like you've had enough go wrong today. Might as well get one thing right."

"No fucking way!" Brett thrilled.

"Fucking way," the shopkeep said solemnly, and then flashed that brown-toothed grin again.

Brett stripped his jacket off and grabbed the hem of his t-shirt, intent on changing right there, but the hippie held up a hand.

"Seventh Veil is a few blocks down. Change in your car, okay? Be well, kid."

"Whatever you say. Thank you. You rule, man."

The old shopkeeper just waved as Brett stumbled out, nearly tripping over his own feet.

Back in the Trans Am, Brett pulled off his t-shirt and put on the Manslaughter shirt. He felt the cotton slide over his chest and marveled at the sensation. Nothing had ever felt this good against his skin, not even Kelly Thompson the last time she was in the backseat.

He angled the rearview mirror to get a good look at himself with the shirt on. It fit him perfectly. From the Manslaughter logo running right across his shoulders down to the hem sitting perfectly above his Iron Maiden belt buckle.

It looked perfect. It *felt* perfect. That knowledge wrapped Brett in a warm blanket and filled his brain with pleasant smoke. All his problems... Money, his future, just trying to get home... None of it seemed to be an issue anymore.

He vaguely remembered that he did need to get home, and decided to try his car again for the hell of it.

He was not surprised that the engine caught on the first try. Nor was he surprised that he reached into the passenger well and found that the Manslaughter cassette had spontaneously restored itself to mint condition.

Everything was just right.

The tape played without issue for the entire ride home, the speakers thundering out an unending fusillade of riffs and shrieking vocals while Brett whizzed up the 101 without hitting even an inch of traffic.

He pulled up in front of his house at the perfect moment, just in time to see mom's boyfriend Gary jogging up the front walkway. Gary, with the salon tan and the sunglasses and the power suits. Gary, who kept offering to set Brett up with a mailroom job at his brokerage.

"Just say the word, sport." Gary was very fond of calling Brett "sport." Almost as fond as he was of fucking Brett's mom.

How fortunate that they could be here together at the same time.

Brett caught up with him just as Gary was at the front door. "Hey. Gary," he called out, scarcely louder than a whisper.

Gary turned with his customary flash of white teeth. "Just getting home, sport?"

The hammer came down before Gary even had time to register what was happening. Brett struck him once, right between the eyes. The hammer made a *crack* as it struck home, and the back of Gary's skull made a bass *thud* as it bounced off the door.

Brett took a breath, cool in and cool out, and watched Gary slump down against the door. The bridge of his sunglasses had broken, letting Brett see the glazed sheen in the dead man's eyes as gravity slowly pulled his body into a crumpled pile on the doorstep.

The hammer, a thing of chipped, pitted wood and rusty iron, hung loosely at his side. Where had it come from? Brett didn't quite know; he just knew that it was certainly lucky that he had it with him. Perfect, really.

From inside the house, his mother called out in response to the skull knocking against the door. "It's open, Gary!"

Brett went inside.

He found his mother in the kitchen, still wearing her tennis outfit as she busied herself with a wine opener in the kitchen. "I don't know when Brett's going to be home," she said without bothering to look up. "We can order in if you want."

Conveniently, Brett now had a pair of six-inch nails to go along with the hammer. Each one was as thick around as his pinkie finger.

He tightened his grip on the hammer and stepped closer.

...Brett's arm throbbed by the time he was finished, but his hard work had paid off. At last, his mother was finally going to stay home where he needed her.

The hammer slipped from his hand, but Brett's mother stayed right where he left her, held up by the twin nails driven through her wrists. She wasn't screaming anymore either. The crunching hammer blow to the larynx had taken care of that.

At long last, everything was just right.

It wasn't until he went to the table with a Coke and a microwave chicken dinner that Brett caught his reflection in the dining room mirror and saw the blood spatters on his Manslaughter t-shirt. That wouldn't do. That wouldn't do at all. "Mom! I need you to wash this!" he called out, pulling the shirt over his head as he did.

The warm fog departed from Brett's mind as quickly as he pulled the t-shirt over his head. Reality hit him harder than he'd hit Gary with the hammer.

And his mother. *His fucking mother.*

His whole body quivered. He ran trembling hands through his hair. *What the fuck? What the fuck did I do?*

"No, no, no." Brett moaned. "Jesus. Jesus fucking..." He spun around in a frantic circle, seeing too much. Christ, too much. Gary sprawled in the doorway. His mother nailed to the wall.

And then the mirror. Brett screamed when he saw what was waiting for him.

It was not his reflection in the glass. It was the old hippie from the shop in Hollywood, leering at him from inside the reflection of his dining room.

"What did I tell you, kid?" The grin was even wider now. "Just right. Just like how I dealt with those MPs when I went AWOL to see Creeps play. Somebody helped me then. Just like I helped you tonight."

The old hippie in the mirror reached toward the glass, and then kept reaching. His hand broke the horizon of the mirror, into the dining room, and closed around Brett's wrist. Too quick to evade. Too powerful to break away from.

"...And now it's your turn," the shopkeeper said.

He pulled, and there was nothing Brett could do. No way to break free. No way to even slow his momentum as he was dragged, screaming, into the surface of the mirror.

Nothing to do but sink into blackness.

...

## 2004

Jodie ran through the pouring rain. There were awnings she could shelter under, but the girl wanted the rain. She welcomed the chill soaking her tank top to her skin, and the thunderous downpour that made it so even she couldn't hear her own wretched sobbing.

Her only wish was that the rain could somehow sweep away the memories from her mind. The memory of Eddie outside the Hammerstein Ballroom with his arms around Megan Taylor, and that slut worming her hands into his jeans right there in line.

*He swore to me,* she moaned. *He SWORE there was nothing going on between them.*

She finally stopped running when at last her lungs simply refused to draw another breath. Jodie sank down onto the curb, heedless of the flashing strobe of headlights driving by through the rain. She sank into the curtain of her soaked, raven dark hair, welcoming the darkness.

*And it had to be TONIGHT!* She had saved up for a month to see Killswitch Engage, and it was ruined now. Absolutely fucking ruined.

"Come on now," a voice called out to her. "I don't know what's the matter, but soaking your ass in New York City pigeon shit soup isn't gonna do you any favors."

*Fuck off, creep.* That was what Jodie was ready to say as she pulled her head out of the darkness of her hair, but she saw the person who'd spoken and was intrigued enough to at least hold off for a moment.

He was in his 50s, lanky and leaning in the doorway of a tiny shop with a wood storefront and dirty glass. He still had a full head of blonde hair, teased out in a massive rat's nest that defied moisture to stay in place. Jodie recognized the Manslaughter t-shirt he wore under his open denim jacket. A little retro for her taste, but they were still a decent group.

He nodded at her Killswitch tank top. "Doors usually open at nine. Why don't you hurry along?"

Jodie wiped her nose and shook her head. "I'm not going," she muttered.

"Not drenched like that, you're not," he agreed laconically. "Come on inside. I think I've got something dry that you'll like."

He drifted back into the store, leaving the door propped open for her to follow. If that was what she wanted to do.

Jodie hesitated. *Stranger danger,* a dull voice warned, but she was used to ignoring that voice. And she really was fucking freezing, now that she had time to think about it.

What the fuck, Jodie got up and approached the tiny store. Her eyes cast up to the sign hanging over the door.

*Just Right Goods,* it said.

As she stepped inside, Jodie could only hope.

## Should I Slay, or Should I Go?
Staci Layne Wilson

*Beckett*

Show 'n Tail was undoubtedly the most unusual strip establishment Zayden Beckett had ever been to. Maybe because it was in Tokyo, where the tech was so cutting edge. The club, which was located in the Shinjuku district, was sleek and angular. It featured a sharp black and silver color scheme, but the roped-off VIP booth was upholstered in soft red leather and had a massive crystal chandelier twinkling above. The ceiling showed strategically exposed pipes and the floor was cement—it was very industrial modern and aligned nicely with his own taste.

The main attraction was the trio of circular stages in the center of the club, each with square Lucite floor tiles that lit up in time to the thumping techno tunes. The shiny stainless-steel poles were being worked constantly by dancers whose moves were truly superhuman. The shapely strippers were athletes beyond compare. Toned to the bone, but with bounces in all the right places, they defied gravity as they spun, twirled, twerked, and shucked their spangled costumes. Some were done up as perverted geishas, while others donned the newly-minted Harajuku styles ranging from gothic Lolita to fairy kei.

Beckett's companions elbowed him with lascivious expressions.

"So, Beckett-San, what do you think of our robot dancers?" asked the younger one, Toma Ito. Ito was an architectural lighting designer who worked for S-K-L, one of the most prestigious concert sound and lighting providers in Asia. The firm had also created the visual wonderland in which they sat.

The older fellow, Kento Tanaka, was one of the CEOs who, hopefully, would agree to work with Beckett on the design and presentation of his next world tour. S-K-L was known for its pioneering work on post-hippie-era stadium rock shows. It provided state-of-the-art sound equipment, laser lighting, props, and even choreography for famous acts beginning with David Bowie and, most recently, Gary Numan.

"They are amazing. I must say, I have never seen anything quite like this." Beckett tore his gaze from the stage and helped himself to some chilled sake and a couple of selections from the impressive spread of sushi and sashimi laid out on the mirrored tabletop.

"I've seen you on Page Six," Tanaka said, referencing the notorious New York Post's gossip column. "Supermodels, lingerie models... ever thought of a robot model?"

Beckett smirked. "Not until now. I didn't even know about this. These, erm, *girls* are so lifelike." Lifelike, and yet, *better* than live. Their smooth, gorgeous faces held neutral, carefree expressions, and their nubile, silicone bodies were flawless.

Ito chortled. "Best of all, you don't have to tip them! No making it rain in these clubs." The man's porous skin was slick with a soused glow, and his hair, despite the expensive salon cut, looked greasy. But his suit, an Armani and obviously custom-tailored, was impeccable.

Beckett felt fine in his dress shirt, tie, slacks, and leather loafers when he'd left the Hilton, but he was somewhat underdressed for Show 'n Tail, as it turned out. The all-male, membership card-carrying clientele were in suits—some three-piece, and all of them overtly expensive. Beckett didn't smoke, and he was in the minority here. Along with the smell of cigarettes, sake, and tea, there was cologne and perhaps a whiff of raging hormones. Looking up at the stage, he wondered if those things gave lap dances.

Beckett took in what Ito had said. But of course, tips would not be necessary. What would robot girls be like in the real world? He thought of all the expensive gifts he'd bought for women in his youth, trying to impress them. What a waste.

Ito popped an entire amaebi sashimi into his mouth and chewed sloppily, oblivious to the withering side-eye from his boss. Talking with his mouth full, he asked if Beckett knew a Tobias Müller.

"The green-energy guy? Yeah. I've heard of him," Beckett replied. He didn't know a thing about Müller, except that he was a billionaire.

"Well, I probably shouldn't be telling you this, but... *sake*!" To illustrate, the designer gulped more down. "Müller-San's company, Pflege-Grün, is supplying power to this new plant in Nevada, which is producing female robots that can do more than just strip."

"You mean they're sex-dolls?" Beckett asked. He suddenly remembered reading an article a year or so ago about humanoid bedroom toys. And the kind of guys who bought them—invalids, hopeless virgins, the socially awkward, shut-ins, and misogynists. Those dolls were just that, though: *dolls*. Inanimate. Lifeless puppets with three holes. Beckett looked up at the lighted stages, each teeming with motion and crackling with charisma.

Robots and dolls really weren't the same thing, were they?

Despite the pounding techno beat, which irked Beckett because it was a blatant rip-off of his signature style, Ito lowered his voice. He leaned in. "I do not understand a lot of the building and programming process, but they're still being patented and no one's supposed to know... I'm an investor." He looked to his boss, and Tanaka gave a brief nod. "So is he. Green energy eco-power plants like Pflege-Grün are the key to keeping manufacturing costs down while maximizing profits. They are going to be big business! Imagine... your every desire can be fulfilled by a charming and sexually adventurous female robot that is lifelike, responsive, warm, and soft to the touch. When you don't want her anymore, you shut her down and put her back into the box. What man wouldn't want one?"

*I would*, Beckett thought. He was tired of the single life, but he couldn't see himself ever marrying. He could do casual relationships, but they always got messy, especially when they demanded to be more than just a road-fling. Not that he had many of those—the fear of catching an STD was just too much for his fastidious psyche to bear. "Sounds intriguing."

"We'll connect you with him," Tanaka said with a sly smile. "That is, if you and I can come to an agreement on your project. Just imagine—our lighting, sound, and decoration, along with robot backup dancers," he gestured to the silicone strippers, "just like these."

...

Three weeks later, Beckett was at the isolated workshop of Dr. Reginald Kasey to tour his facility. It was, as his Japanese associates said, top secret. He'd had to sign three non-disclosure agreements before Kasey would even speak to him.

The lab was located about six miles outside Las Vegas, and it was hidden underground. A little weird, but nothing much surprised Beckett anymore. He'd been around the block more than a time or two. He was older than his fans knew—with his neon lids, draped blush, steel-gray painted mouth, sculpted platinum hair, and oversized Kansai Yamamoto suits, it was impossible to tell his age when he was onstage.

Once his Maserati was parked inside the above-ground, non-descript warehouse as instructed, Beckett followed the directions which had been messengered to him that morning. There was a lone elevator near the center of the warehouse, which was summoned by the touch of a button. It had only one direction: Down.

Beckett glanced at himself in the elevator's mirrored interior, thinking he was looking tired. He couldn't wait to get back on the road—that's where his spark came from. But he was pleased that he was still as lean and chiseled as he'd been in his 20s. He worked hard to maintain his physique, defying the many sedentary hours the composing of his computer-generated music demanded and the sleepless nights that sapped his energy. His stern, handsome face was narrow, bordering on gaunt, and while there was a bit of a sag to his jawline now, his eyes remained a fierce, saturated green. He looked "ambitious," he'd been told. He took it as a compliment.

The elevator came to a smooth stop, then the metal doors parted. The lobby was clearly under construction. Dust motes danced on the thick, stuffy air, and clear plastic sheeting hung from bare beams. Some walls were in, but they weren't finished yet. There were no workmen. No chairs. However, there was a receptionist stationed at a hospital-like podium at the far end of the room.

She smiled at Beckett, showing off even white teeth framed by pouty, scarlet lips. "Good afternoon! You must be Zayden Beckett."

He crossed the room. "I am."

The young woman introduced herself as Linda. She was platinum blonde and had a welcoming smile. She asked him to sign in, and once he did, she led him into a nearby waiting room. Her high heels made loud, but not unpleasant, click-clack sounds on the concrete floor.

The small chamber was in disarray as well, but at least there were some chairs and a table with a carafe of coffee and mugs bearing Kasey's Femme-Droid logo. The shapely silver silhouette echoed the famous "mud-flap girl" seen on the backends of big trucks everywhere, but this figure was standing and resting her hands on an F and a D.

"Please, sit," Linda said. Her voice was beautiful, like the sound of gentle bells. Beckett did so, and as if on cue, a viewing screen slid down from the ceiling. "We have a film for you to watch—just a short one—and then I shall take you to Dr. Kasey." The lights dimmed, and Linda left.

Beckett watched the screen as a mosaic of effigies was revealed in a series of still photos and painted imagery. It was a timeline, beginning with prehistoric dolls made of rag, clay, wax, and wood. Then they showed porcelain models used by physicians and small Greek statues. Next came the very first Japanese automatons—these were the mechanized Karakuri puppets made from the 17th century to the 19th century. From that, the film segued into images of walking, talking French maid dolls once popular in Marie Antoinette's court, then marionettes that commanded the stage. These led to film clips of prototype robots, crude blow-up sex dolls, and cartoonish androids. This was followed by quick clips from sci-fi movies such as *Metropolis*, *Dr. Goldfoot and the Bikini Machine*, the more-recent *Galaxina,* and a few others he didn't recognize. The story then flowed into a montage of stills showing ladies of all shapes, sizes, and ethnicities, from the 1920s to futuristic, fantastical guesses as to how womanhood might evolve further.

The fast-paced medley picked up speed until Beckett felt woozy and thought he might be sick.

Finally, relief was granted in the sanctuary of a single, drop-dead gorgeous face. The woman, blonde-haired and blue-eyed, seemed to be looking back at him. The camera slowly inched in, closer, closer, until Beckett was in her left eye, through her pupil, and finally, to her magnificent mechanical brain. The voice of a narrator came in, extolling the patented Femme-Droid's virtues and how she would be the most important invention to be unveiled in the late-20th century.

The short film ended a few minutes later, and the lights snapped on.

Linda was standing at his side, smiling down at him. "Dr. Kasey will see you now."

She led him through a corridor with exposed beams and plastic sheeting, and advised him to watch his step.

Kasey's laboratory seemed to be the only finished chamber in the underground compound. It was awash in white, from its shiny tile flooring to its textured ceilings beaming with recessed lights. As Beckett followed the receptionist through the tunnel-like corridor which led to the lab, he was stunned to see row after row of perfect, beautiful, sexy, inanimate robot women lining the walls. There were dozens of them— mostly finished and clothed, but some were nude, bald, and in various stages of assembly.

At the end of the hallway, at the far end of the large workshop, was a single human occupant: Dr. Reginald Kasey. He was seated at a clear Lucite desk and was jabbing away at the keyboard to a large computer, clearly engrossed in his work. He wore nondescript medical scrubs, a white coat, and thick glasses. He didn't look up at the sound of Linda and Beckett's footfalls, and when she announced him, Kasey flinched. Then he grinned, gecko-like.

"Zayden Beckett! What a pleasure to have you here. Welcome, welcome!" Kasey stood and crossed the room with short, quick steps.

Linda stepped aside as the men shook hands.

Beckett found Kasey's bones limp and his flesh damp. "Thank you," he said, fighting the urge to wipe his palm on his pant leg.

Kasey smiled again, revealing distinct spaces between his rather large teeth. They resembled white piano keys. "May we get you a cappuccino? Brandy? Cigar?" Even his voice sounded moist.

Beckett shook his head. "No, thanks."

"Busy man!" Kasey gushed obsequiously. "I know, I know! I cannot tell you how closely I've followed your career. I'm such a fan. A self-made man like you, you're an inspiration to us all!"

Beckett doubted such a dweeb listened to *his* sophisticated music. Then again, his early '80s hit *Software for Hardware* was impossible to miss these days. The Apple Macintosh SE TV commercial using the song as its theme had debuted during the Super Bowl, thus putting it back in heavy rotation on the nation's radio stations.

Beckett nodded a curt thanks, then looked around the room. In addition to the Femme-Droids lining the hallway walls, there were two on metal gurneys and a few more lying on the ground near Kasey's desk. Floating shelves held inventories of hands, heads, eyes, wigs, and other interchangeable body parts.

Kasey, clearly uncomfortable with Beckett's silence, filled the gap. "You have it all," he gushed. "Success, style, intellect, and, heh-heh… money. Lots of money."

"Just to be clear, I don't *need* a Femme-Droid. I want one. Tobias Müller told me it's a great investment. If I like what I see, I may purchase several to be part of the stage show for my '88 world tour."

"Understood, Mr. Beckett. And yes, it's the opportunity of a lifetime. You will not be disappointed! We can program them to dance in perfect time to all of your hits—*Sushi Dragonflies, Orange Jumpsuit, Shadow Self…* you name it. Backup vocals, too." Kasey glanced at Linda, then back to Beckett. "Are you sure, no cappuccino? Our Kopi Luwak beans are double roasted over a low flame right here in the lab by specially programmed Femme-Droid baristas."

There was a small kitchenette to the far right of the chamber. Beckett spotted two Femme-Droids wearing nothing but lingerie, tending to a coffeemaker so elaborate it looked as though one would require an engineering degree just to turn it on.

Beckett knew what Kopi Luwak was. The coffee was brewed from beans that had traversed the gastrointestinal tract of an Asian palm civet—in other words, shat out, then harvested. Basically, it was cat-poop cappuccino, and Beckett couldn't think of anything he'd want in his mouth less. "No thanks."

"Understandable," Kasey replied. "How about good old hand-roasted, single-origin, fair trade organic beans? Do you take cream? Ours is from grass-fed cattle from ethical farmers who eschew antibiotics and hormones. Our friend Müller insists that everything here, and I do mean *everything*, is eco-friendly." A micro-expression of annoyance tweaked his features. When Beckett shook his head, the doctor smiled and went on. "Tea, then? We have jasmine leaves from the Ming Dynasty, excavated from ruins dating back to 1544. It's"—he kissed his fingertips for emphasis—"delicious!"

"Okay, whatever." Anything to shut this guy up. "Two sugars."

Kasey gave a heavy sigh of relief and satisfaction. Even though he lived among robots, he was clearly a people-pleaser. He turned to Linda. "Help them."

The receptionist gave a single nod and joined the baristas. Beckett noticed a glide to her gait, different from what it was outside the lab. Her heels didn't clack. He turned to the doctor. "Is she...?"

Kasey grinned. "Yep. A Femme-Droid. You would never have known, would you?"

"Impressive."

"Thank you! If I may say so myself, my invention has surpassed even my own wildest expectations. They can be fueled in the usual way, but the eco-power seems to imbue them with special qualities. It does come from nature, after all. Perhaps there's inexplicable alchemy at play? I consider myself lucky I was able to talk Tobias into this, well, rather *unusual* endeavor." He sniggered. "And thank *you* for investing!"

Beckett held up a hand, palm out. "I can't fully commit until I've tried one. I need to know exactly what I'm getting into. It's the same with my music—I would never write a song that I myself wouldn't want to listen to."

"Totally understandable, Mr. Beckett. And smart. Very prudent. While there are other robots and droids in development all over the world, ours are special because they're the greenest red-hot sex goddesses on the planet!"

Linda returned with tea for both men. She seemed less human now, her expression a blank. Beckett wondered if she was powering down.

Kasey went on with his sales pitch. "These babies are going to revolutionize the world. As you know, they are the only solar-fueled, eco-energized girls available, and I alone hold the patent."

Beckett cautiously sipped at the piping hot tea. "Maybe I've seen too many sci-fi horror movies, but... can these things malfunction? Are they at all dangerous?"

Kasey's muddy brown, toad-like eyes lit up with sinister glee. "Well," he slyly drew out the word, "there is a bit of morbid trivia about the very first human being ever to have been murdered by a machine. It happened six years ago when a worker was tinkering on a broken robot at a Kawasaki plant in Japan. He failed to turn it off completely, and the poor fellow met a rather grisly end when the robot went haywire and pushed him into a grinding machine. But the only kind of grinding our Femme-Droids do is groin-to-groin, you know?" The inventor laughed and winked.

Beckett gestured to the marvelous machines working in the kitchenette. "Tell me more about the experience their owners will have."

Kasey led Beckett to his desk and gestured to his small, boxy computer screen, which was blazing with green, gleaming streaming code. With one touch of a key, the code coalesced, then formed the classic hourglass shape of a woman. Skin coated the simulated machine, then features, hair, and a slinky dress completed the look. "Femme-Droid has an operating system more advanced than anything else to date," Kasey explained. "She learns from every experience and will adapt to her person in order to please him to the fullest. What's more, she has a reward system built into her circuitry. It actually feels good to her when she has sex… it's kind of like how your computer runs better when all its software is up to date, you know?"

Beckett inhaled, noticing a sweet smell that was even stronger than the jasmine and brown sugar emanating from the teacups. "What is that? Cotton candy?"

"That's the Femme-Droid aroma. She also generates her a unique signature scent, much like a real woman. There is a touch of sweetness we've added to our specially patented platinum silicone. Come get a whiff," invited Kasey, leading Beckett to four inanimate, fully completed, and scantily-dressed Femme-Droids. Their eyes were open in vacant stares, and their full, pouty lips were slightly parted. "Smell… right here," Kasey said, indicating the nearest one's mouth. "Her breath is spun sugar."

Beckett nodded, taking it all in and letting Kasey talk. In the course of building his empire, he had learned that the less he said, the more others talked. And when they talked, they usually revealed things. He was indeed ready, willing, and able to invest—especially if it meant allying with the uber-rich and super-trendy Müller—but the Femme-Droids still needed to pass the smell-test. So to speak.

"These," Kasey said, "are the prototypes from which all the variations are made. We have The Sweetheart, The Wife, The Mistress, and The Call Girl."

Beckett couldn't see much difference between the models. The Sweetheart and The Wife were less showy but still knockouts. The Mistress and The Call Girl were more exaggerated in their figures, with large, round beachball breasts made to look like implants. They all had delicate hands, tiny feet, and slim hips. The sweet, sugary scent was strangely arousing, even in this clinical setting.

Beckett stepped back and finished his tea. The instant he lowered the cup from his mouth, a Femme-Droid appeared and took it from him. She drifted back to the kitchenette without a word. Beckett looked at his watch. "When is Müller going to be here?"

As if on cue, Müller rushed in, breathless. "Forgive me, gentlemen! My driver was late." He spoke with a nearly-quashed German accent.

Beckett noted that Müller was well-dressed but not ostentatiously so. He guessed the suit was made of hemp. "Don't they have self-driving cars yet?"

The green-energy guru shook hands with Beckett, then Kasey. Müller wiped his newly-clammy hand on his pantleg, then replied, "They're already here. A man called Ernst Dickmanns put a driverless Mercedes onto the roads of Europe in 1984—appropriately enough—but it never really caught on. I predict it will, eventually. I'm investing in that tech as well." He smiled, revealing slightly discolored teeth. Beckett suspected that the man used some sort of ineffective, all-natural toothpaste. "But first, the Femme-Droid. Thanks for coming, Mr. Beckett. And Reginald, I cannot believe the progress you've made since I was last here! The Femme-Droids are gorgeous! Especially Flynn. Wow."

Beckett's eyebrows shot up. "Flynn?"

The inventor nodded. "Yes, she is our flagship model in the sex line. This is just the first step, to... for lack of a better word, *whet* the appetites of the American public for robotic servants. Femme-Droids, and later our Boy-Bots, will do all the jobs humans don't want to, or can't, do. They will work assembly lines, dig ditches, direct traffic, enforce the law, go to war... but I'm getting ahead of myself. The basic idea is to start with a kiss." Kasey held out his empty teacup, which was quickly collected by a female figure and spirited away. "Tea, Reginald?" When Müller shook his head, Kasey went on. "Why don't we take a look at Flynn?"

The men walked over a few steps to a nearby model, and Kasey flicked an unseen switch behind her ear to activate her.

Flynn stepped forward, coming very close to Beckett. Barefoot and draped in a micro-mini toga, she was a timeless beauty. Her hair and makeup were flawless, and he could even see minute pores in her synthetic skin. She looked exactly like the genuine article, but her arms stayed slack at her sides, and her face was void of expression.

The inventor sighed with professional pride. "Watch this, Mr. Beckett." Kasey removed a remote control from the front pocket of his lab coat and pressed a few buttons. The Femme-Droid came to life, her countenance and movements miming the things the inventor was saying.

"The Femme-Droid will never be boring, because she has several interactive sexual programs. She can be a virgin."

Flynn averted her eyes and brought her arms in, shyly covering her chest.

"Submissive."

She dropped her arms and held them out in invitation, smiling sweetly.

"Seductive."

She beckoned with one finger, encouraging Beckett to come to her.

"Wanton."

She tossed her hair and caressed her body with lust.

"Giving."

Her expression turned convincingly inviting.

"Aggressive," Kasey continued.

She channeled a classic sex kitten, thrusting her chest out and stamping one foot.

"She can be an erudite high-class prostitute or a drugged-out street whore."

Flynn stood up straight, the picture of posh breeding. She gave Beckett a slight come-hither smile. Then she drooped, and her expression conveyed utter hopelessness.

Kasey pressed the remote one more time, and Flynn returned to her neutral state. "The choice is yours, Mr. Beckett. Whatever you might want on any given day, she will be just that. She simulates, then stimulates. She gyrates, pulsates, vibrates, and satiates."

He was sold. "Have Flynn shipped to my private residence."

...

Sex with Flynn was... interesting. It was more than masturbation but less than being with a woman. He was fascinated by how lively—and lifelike—the Femme-Droid was while in the act and how, with a flick of the switch behind her left ear, she would turn completely off. There was something about this on-off power he suddenly had that both repulsed and captivated him. In any case, it could create an interesting onstage dynamic. He soon cast aside the backup-dancers idea—

he would be the first musician to have an all-android band.

For now, it—*she*, he reminded himself—spent hours on end locked away in his bedroom closet. He'd turned her off, but oddly, Flynn's eyes stayed open in a fixed gaze when he did so. It was unnerving, to say the least.

Fortunately, his new friend Müller was the perfect companion when it came to discussing the pros and cons of the Femme-Droid venture. The first time Müller came by, it was ostensibly to check on Flynn, but Beckett suspected that the green-energy mogul had just wanted to see what kind of house the "famous rock star" had. Many people wondered about such things, and surely, Beckett assumed, Tobias Müller was no exception.

His home was atypical of the usual Las Vegas architecture, which ranged from glitzy to ghastly. The outside vibe flowed into the living quarters. The rooms were angular, glassy, and sleek. Cubist sculptures and geometric shapes lined the shelves in addition to the requisite books and a collection of board games. During his tour, Müller had instantly spotted Go—it was the world's most ancient and complex game, and Beckett was impressed that the energy expert even knew what it was.

According to legend, Go was created as a teaching tool when the Chinese Emperor Yao designed it for his son to learn discipline, concentration, and balance. Other sources said Go was an ancient fortune-telling device used by astrologers. While it was probably the latter, Beckett preferred the first scenario. It appealed to his no-nonsense mindset.

The press had dubbed him "Nexus 6" after the androids in sci-fi icon Philip K. Dick's novel *Do Androids Dream of Electric Sheep?* because he was a laser-focused, hyper-competitive, overachieving Type-A who single-mindedly decimated any and all competitors.

Underneath the living quarters was a state-of-the-art recording studio. His pride and joy was his Lexicon 480L Digital Effects System, which had cost more than some of his cars. He also had a Pultec outboard, a Trident console, an Alesis Midiverb, three organs, two drum machines, Sennheiser and Shure mics, plus an array of electric and acoustic guitars, though he seldom used real instruments anymore.

Beckett sat at the bar with a glass of buttercream chardonnay while Müller stuck with the German beer he'd brought. They played a game of Go and talked about the many potential benefits of Kasey's Femme-Droids, including abolishing unwanted pregnancies, which had naturally led the two childless men to the topic of what they saw as much-needed population control.

"Do you realize," he said as he moved his white stone to one of the grids, "that during the 20th century alone, the world's population grew from 1.65 billion to over five billion? The United States is third after China and India as the reproduction culprits. It makes me sick, quite frankly."

Müller took a quick gulp of his beer as if punctuating Beckett's disgust. "That's where the experiment comes in. Sex without consequence."

"That's part of it, sure. From the fall of the Roman Empire to Columbus stumbling upon America, it took 13 centuries to build up to a population of 200 million. Now, it takes only two years! Pasteurization, inoculation, you name it... what's helped us thrive is going to keep us from surviving. Not unless we can get this experiment, and us, into space." He'd been thinking about the possibilities beyond this initial investment—not to mention his music career, which couldn't last forever in these fickle times—and they excited him. "Truly: this planet is just a black hole waiting to happen. We are headed for an event horizon."

Müller turned to look at him. He moved one of his black stones without looking down at the board. "The point of no return? You really think so? In the here and now, Earth is the only home we've got. We've got to preserve it. Take care of it. Keep it green."

"True enough. But the hard, cold fact is: we are destroying Earth. How much of the Brazilian Rain Forest is gone now? You know that better than anyone. And you're trying to reverse our damage. I appreciate it, but eventually, it won't be enough. Tobias, living on other planets will be the only way for us to go on as a species. This one won't be habitable forever. And our so-called selfish genes? They've got to be fixed." *Not that I'm giving up mine*, he thought. "Biochemists have done some ground-breaking work, but it won't solve our problem. Centuries of evolutionary traits can't be changed with just a few splices. Not yet."

"I don't know if it's possible. It still feels unreal to me."

Beckett chuckled. "Says the man who is staking everything on Femme-Droids. Talk about unreal! It *is* possible—more than possible. But any hope of space settlement will require cost-effective and safe launch systems to deliver thousands, maybe even millions, of people into orbit. And then planetary colonization."

Müller opened another beer. "Millions?"

"Look at it this way: a hundred years ago nobody had ever flown in an airplane, but today over a billion people hop aboard every year. And think about the other aspects. But there could be settlements at zero-G making wheelchairs and walkers a thing of the past. Escape-proof prisons could be put in orbit. The possibilities are endless."

"A floating bordello, where one's wife would never find him..." Müller changed the subject. "Tell me how you're liking Flynn. I'm sure Reginald is dying to know."

Beckett's brow knitted. "She's..."

"Have you had her turned on for more than just playtime?"

"Not really. I feel silly talking to it."

"Her."

Beckett shrugged, then finished his wine. He examined the grid, figuring out his next move. Müller wasn't much of an opponent, but it felt good to be playing.

"Do you think a human could fall in love with a robot?" asked Müller. There was an edge to his tone that made the question seem more than just rhetorical.

Beckett figured Müller must have a Femme-Droid of his own at home. "Hm. Why not flip that around and ask if a robot could fall in love with a human?"

"I guess that depends on how one defines love," Müller replied. "Is it the feeling of excitement you get from being with that person, or is it more about the feeling of excitement you know they feel when they're with *you*? That can be very powerful, can't it?

Knowing that you could break a heart—or a circuit board—at your whim." He moved one of his prisoners, then looked to Beckett for approval.

"Not bad." He moved his piece onto an intersection. "I think you're reading way too much into this, Tobias."

"Or maybe not enough. After all, you can't have artificial intelligence without *intelligence*. Is it right, or even ethical, to intellectualize something as ephemeral as love?"

Beckett examined his fingernails. He hated talking about feelings. Always had, always would. "In any case, Flynn's time here is up."

"Which one will you try next?"

...

Beckett didn't want to go back to the lab to choose another model. Though he couldn't put his finger on it, there was something a little off about that place, and it gave him the creeps.

With the inventor on speakerphone, he paged quickly through Kasey's catalog of Femme-Droids. A bevy of beauties went by in a blur.

Beckett stopped on one called Tatiana. The Tatiana model was shown from all angles, and she was a knockout. Red hair, big brown doe eyes, full lips, and stacked to the max. She looked almost cartoonish, which appealed to him. Flynn was disconcertingly lifelike. Last night, after using her, he could have sworn her eyes flicked up at him as the closet door closed.

"I like this one called Tatiana," he announced. "The text says she's a special Russian Nesting Doll... what does that mean?"

Kasey's voice sounded phlegmy, even over the miles of wires. "Well, she's Russian. Accent, the whole bit. But in her patented lady parts are various levels of adjustment. So, like an actual Russian Nesting Doll, she starts off normal-sized, then gets smaller and smaller inside, until she feels like a virgin. I guess you could say it's like reverse-engineering."

Beckett was intrigued. "Sounds... unique."

"Oh, trust me! She is. She's one-of-a-kind. I don't even have a backup yet. Tatiana is an upgrade over Flynn because she can emit bio-electrical currents, which trigger pleasant feelings in a human and sends an endorphin rush to his brain. It's a bit different from the cotton candy aroma lure."

"Okay. And please make sure this one's eyes close when it's powered down. Flynn gives me the creeps when it's shut off. It just stares at me."

"Hmm. Must be a bug. Sorry about that. You *are* putting her in a cool, dark place when she's not in use, right?"

"The closet in my bedroom. I keep it locked. Don't want the housekeeper to see..."

"Why don't I add a program to Tatiana so she can replace your maid?"

"No, thanks. Look, Kasey. I've got to go," Beckett snapped. A rush of dislike for the weirdo scientist flooded him. "Just take care of this. As soon as I'm satisfied with what I'm getting, and once we go over the contracts again, you'll get your money."

...

Tatiana arrived the next day.

Beckett answered the door and was met by a strapping delivery man in plain, gray overalls. On the front pocket was small, embroidered script reading "Kasey Laboratories." At his side was an industrial dolly with a large, oblong box perched precariously on its ledge. It was tied with three bungee cords. The man gave a curt smile. "Got a delivery here for you, Mr. Beckett, and a pick-up."

"Yes. Would you mind wheeling that into my office? The pick-up is in there too."

"No worries, sir."

Beckett could have sworn he caught a conspiratorial smirk on the man's face, but the look was gone before it could set. He didn't like the idea of this guy knowing what he was up to... and, he guessed, Kasey's employee had sampled the wares himself. He shuddered inwardly, hoping that Tatiana was clean and disinfected. He assumed that she, same as Flynn, would arrive with a sanitary seal, cleaning solution, and instructions.

He opened the container with considerable effort. Tatiana lay on her back, arms at her sides and feet crossed at the ankles. Her eyes were, thankfully, closed. On her rosebud mouth was a slight smile. She was dressed in black lingerie, and just beside her head, folded neatly, were instructions.

Beckett flicked the switch behind her ear, and Tatiana sighed sweetly as if waking from a lovely dream. The effigy's eyes fluttered open, their long lashes sweeping, catlike, to the outer corners. Her fingers twitched, then one hand came up. He took it and helped the Femme-Droid to her feet.

Once righted, Tatiana immediately put her arms around her new master and started kissing him. He stumbled backwards at Tatiana's onslaught, then put his hands on her hips. Her skin was already warm. So was her tongue. Beckett was taken aback for just a moment, and then he went with it.

An hour later, he was spent. He lay on the rug, flat on his back, panting. His heart raced. He'd never felt such intense physical pleasure in his life. He felt the Femme-Droid's hand gliding southward. Again. "No," he gasped. "Tatiana, stop! I can't take any more."

The automaton had, as Dr. Kasey promised, a heavy Russian accent. "But why? I love you, Zayden."

Beckett's body stiffened in every joint but one. "Uh-uh. No *love*, and no *Zayden*." He sat up, then reached for the instructions. He read them, finding them more advanced than Flynn's had been. He pressed a recessed button next to the switch concealed behind her ear. "Instruction sequence commence: Tatiana will *desire* Zayden Beckett. Tatiana will not use the word *love*. Tatiana will refer to Zayden Beckett only as *Beckett*. End instruction sequence."

Tatiana went rigid and blinked rapidly, absorbing her orders. Then she relaxed and smiled. "Beckett," she said. "I desire you."

"Thank you. But for now, you'll have to behave. I'll show you where you sleep." While he felt a bit silly talking to the robot as if it were alive, or even a pet, Kasey had explained to him that Femme-Droids needed verbal feedback to update. It was an essential part of their programming, and, the inventor insisted, it was important on the consumer side of things, as well. If people didn't become close to their Femme-Droids, even emotionally attached, then they wouldn't keep buying, or at least upgrading them. Beckett wanted to test it out, to monitor her responses, even if it did make him feel rather ridiculous.

He fixed his clothes, then straightened her teddy. He beckoned Tatiana to follow him, and, doglike, she heeled him across the hall and up the stairs until they reached the walk-in closet of his bedroom. He opened the door, then motioned her inside. She did as she was instructed. He sat her down in a chair at the far end, then flicked the switch behind her ear. Tatiana's eyes closed, and he caught an almost imperceptible whirring sound as she shut down. Beckett looked at her for a long moment.

"This is crazy," he said with a wince. "And painful." He hadn't felt so battered since his college days.

He closed the closet door, and without returning to his office to shut off the lights, he fell into bed. He was exhausted. But he found he could not sleep. His mind raced, and he felt strangely giddy. Giddy was not a word associated with Zayden Beckett... ever. His thoughts pinged here and there, like caged birds longing for the freedom of the open sky; they flapped about but never flew.

A few hours later, after catching only a few fitful winks, he couldn't resist taking another go at Tatiana. It was almost as if she was willing him to come to her. *Not possible, of course. I'm the one making the decisions here.*

Three days later, he wasn't so sure. He found himself thinking obsessively about Tatiana when she was stored away. When she wasn't, he couldn't stop touching her, marveling at her softness and warmth. He found himself inhaling her aroma as if it were a drug. He even wanted to talk to her, to know what she... *thought.*

As it turned out, she didn't think of anything but sex. Which was fine at first blush, but Beckett was disconcerted by his response to the Femme-Droid. He'd never been so preoccupied and certainly had never become hooked on anything. He prided himself on his analytical mind and self-control. While he had to admire Dr. Kasey's programming abilities—surely the constant positive feedback he was getting from Tatiana was triggering his endorphins—he felt uneasy.

With Tatiana shut down and stashed away, Beckett made a call to Kasey from his office and told him he wanted to send her back sooner rather than later.

"But I don't understand, Mr. Beckett. Tatiana is perfect!" Kasey sputtered.

"Too perfect. Explain to me again this thing that she does with my endorphins."

"The Tatiana model sends special bioelectrical currents from her erotic emission zone, which signals your endorphins to rush. It's all physiological. I assure you, Mr. Beckett, there's nothing harmful about it."

"Feels like mind control to me, Kasey. I can't stop thinking about her, er, it."

"Are you saying you're falling in *love* with Tatiana?" There was a note of intrigue in Kasey's tone as if this was a development he had hoped for.

"Of course not! Please. Me, in love with a robot. I am my own man, and no machine is going to interfere with my free will. That might be okay for the average consumer, but not me."

"Of course. I have many other models to choose from. I even have a few that don't speak at all. Would that be better?"

"Actually, I have some unique specifications. Can you build me a Femme-Droid made to order?"

There was a silence, then: "For a price. Not to sound mercenary, but unlike yourself and Mr. Müller, I am not rich. I'm waiting on the," he paused as if searching for the right word, "capital. I cannot launch until everything is in place."

"Well, here's what I have in mind," Beckett said. "A dual-purpose machine. One that can be in my band *and* attend events with me.

When I walk a red carpet, I need someone beautiful and charming at my side."

There had been speculation in the music press as to why he never went anywhere with anyone, and much as it made him grit his teeth, he knew appearances were important. This year's MTV Music Awards had been especially embarrassing.

Peter Gabriel won ten awards, including the Video Vanguard Award and Video of the Year for his video *Sledgehammer*, and he'd shattered Beckett's own VMA record for most Moonmen garnered in a single night. Gabriel also had the most stunning women swooning, while Beckett was utterly alone, which raised snarky questions about his sexuality from the VJs. Frankly, he was tired of it, and the more he thought about practical uses for his Femme-Droid, the more its potential adaptability appealed to him.

"Mr. Beckett, with all due respect, you must realize that the Femme-Droid is for indoor use only at this time. Someday we will have them in the workplace, in public—or in space, as you suggested—but it's early in their development. You could have them on stage with you, but climate control is crucial. I know they seem versatile, but there are... limitations." Sounding as though he realized he might be making his potential investor doubt the venture, Kasey quickly added, "But that is concerning the first wave only. As I said when you were here for the tour, it starts with a kiss. After the public is comfortable with having Femme-Droids and Boy-Bots in their homes, we will introduce models that can interact reliably with more than one user at a time."

"What about your receptionist and your baristas?"

"Those are programmed to follow simple tasks in response to only a few likely scenarios. Linda was fed information about you and Tobias. If a stranger had somehow managed to crack our codes and find his or her way into the lab, she would not react. And I only have the coffee and a few kinds of tea on hand. If you'd gone to one of them and asked for hot chocolate—well, I'm not sure how they would have responded."

"I have faith in you. So much so, that I am willing to invest even more than you initially asked. Wouldn't it be something for me to take one out for a spin, say to an important, high-profile event, then reveal to the world later that my date was one of *your* inventions?"

"Well… I guess…"

"Perfect. I've been invited to a black-tie *Rolling Stone* gala next week."

"Next week?! To create a specially made Femme-Droid to order? I can't…"

Beckett named the figure he would invest on top of the previously proposed amount. "*Now* can you?"

*Kasey*

Kasey stared at the phone for a moment after realizing he'd been hung up on. "How am I going pull this off?" he muttered. Sweat prickled his palms. This venture was not getting off to the smoothest start, but he had to go with it.

The scientist had worked for so many years on his Femme-Droids in lonely obscurity. First in the Midwest, then Aogashima Island in Japan where he'd met Tobias Müller, and now here in this godforsaken desert. While the isolation and time had allowed him to make a lot of progress, he knew that his products couldn't truly take off until they belonged to the world. Someday soon, the marketplace would dictate what constituted perfection.

The *marketplace*. The thought of going public both thrilled and terrified him. If everything went the way he hoped, he would be vindicated. Those asshole colleagues who'd blackballed him for so-called unethical misconduct would be begging to work with him. *Begging!*

He didn't like the way the famous rock star was pushing him around, though. As if having money and needs was more important than anything else. Kasey had to be very careful with the Femme-Droid line—the repair of his reputation, not to mention the chance to stun the world, meant so much to him. It meant everything, really. But he also couldn't afford to upset Zayden Beckett, not with the planned launch approaching. He'd been in hiding so long... he could almost taste the freedom and the fame.

Kasey let his mind wander to a daydream. His Femme-Droids on the lighted stage as the height of Beckett's live extravaganza. He hadn't been lying when he said he was a fan. Although meeting the taciturn artist had been a letdown, he still loved the music. With its throbbing, stabbing chunks of synthesizer riffs, stark arrangements, and detached vocals augmented by a Moog vocoder, it put him in the perfect mood to design and create. In fact, it had been Beckett's Asian aesthetic that had led him to study in Japan and immerse himself in the culture and technology—though he didn't dare share that tidbit with Beckett or Müller. Kasey certainly didn't want to be perceived as some crazy fan, but he knew he would be the perfect person to supply Beckett with the Femme-Droid band for his upcoming '88 tour. And beyond. He could imagine the guys from Kraftwerk wanting their own models, and maybe even Madonna or Michael Jackson. The possibilities were beyond thrilling.

Kasey called Müller, who picked up before the first ring finished its trill.

"Yes, Reginald?"

"I am so sorry, Tobias, but... Beckett wants another Femme-Droid."

"So, what's the problem? We told him he'd get three samples. We need him. Send another over."

"But he wants a specially-made model. A prototype. One of a kind."

"I repeat: What's the problem? Beckett is a serious investor."

"He needs her in less than a week. And he wants to take the droid... out in public. It's a *Rolling Stone* party. After talking with him, I looked it up and it is a huge event. Very high-profile. This could be a PR nightmare if anyone learns too soon that his date is a robot. I think we need more time."

Müller sighed. There was a long silence, then: "I see."

Kasey and Müller had known each other for over a year now, but the inventor couldn't quite grasp what those two words meant. They sounded ominous.

"Well, I know we didn't want to get ahead of ourselves, but I have some bad news. The Japanese investors have backed out."

"What?"

"Don't worry. The private club is still using the pole dancers and paying their rental fee. But Tanaka and Ito have changed their minds."

"Why?"

"Reginald, listen to me. You have to give Beckett what he wants, but you must be very, very precise. No cutting corners. Everything has to be green. One hundred percent eco-friendly. Hang tight. I'm coming over."

...

An hour later, Kasey and Müller were standing before an assortment of Femme-Droids. Some were in pieces or only partially assembled, as Kasey had been mixing and matching to see if there was some way he could fool Beckett into thinking he was getting something brand new. But none of the faces were quite right.

"What about Lexi, here?" Müller asked.

"Oh, no... please don't make me part with Lexi. Besides, as I told you, Mr. Beckett said he wants it made from scratch, just for him. He messengered the specifications over, and it's the tallest order I have ever seen. He even sent a sketch of what he wants her to look like."

"An actress? We can't do that—we don't have the licensing for famous likenesses. Yet."

"No, not anyone I recognize. Probably an ex. I'm okay with that. All the world's greatest artists worked from live models... except maybe Picasso in his abstract period. Though sometimes, a third breast would be nice," Kasey sniggered.

"What's so special about Lexi that you can't part with her?"

"Lexi is the best. She is my assistant for assembly here in the lab, my cook in the kitchen, and my *yūjo* in the bedroom." Kasey took a remote control from his pocket and pointed it at the Femme-Droid. Lexi stepped forward. "Good morning, Lexi."

"Good morning, Master."

Müller looked askance at Kasey.

Kasey reddened. "It's our thing."

"I guess it's harmless. After all, we *want* these things to be demeaned in place of real women. That's part of their purpose—let *them* be the strippers and the prostitutes, right?"

Kasey didn't reply. Of course, that was part of the ultimate plan. At least, he thought so. Originally, Tobias wanted the eco-friendly droids and bots made strictly for doing chores, working assembly lines, and other menial tasks. It had taken a lot of persuading to get him to come around to considering their baser purpose, but his bitter divorce had been the turning point. That, and the addictive, intoxicating component Kasey added to the Femme-Droid line in more recent upgrades.

It wasn't like Dr. Kasey didn't tell his investors about the signature scent. He simply left out the "addictive" part. He also didn't tell them about the hidden cameras... perfect for blackmailing purposes, if ever needed. Kasey always had an ace in the hole. Someday, he thought, his creations could be Femme-Droid fatales—sexy, spying war machines. But one thing at a time. First, secure Beckett's investment. Second, get them onstage. Then, world domination.

The inventor turned his attention to back Lexi, who was standing before them expectantly, like a shapely word processor with big, blinking blue eyes in the place of a flashing cursor.

"She is really something. You sure you don't want to part with her? Maybe just her torso?" asked Müller, admiring her curves. He looked around the room, and then sighed. "I've only met Beckett a few times, but he strikes me as an extremely exacting man. He's not going to accept a half-assed Femme-Droid."

"But all of my creations are beyond reproach," Kasey protested.

"Now, now." Müller put a reassuring hand on his partner's narrow, bony shoulder. "I'm not implying they aren't. But he is not easy to please, obviously. I mean, you sent two perfectly made, state-of-the-art, gorgeous models to him, and he wasn't satisfied with either one." He bit his lower lip, thinking. "With Tanaka and Ito out, we need Beckett more than ever if we're going to meet our deadline."

"But it's only a self-imposed deadline. Can't we—"

"No. It absolutely has to be January 1, 1988."

...

At first, Kasey thought he could deliver. He'd been confident. Cocky, even. But the night before the gala, he realized he was in big trouble.

He was being squeezed from both ends— Müller and Beckett were checking in with him constantly, demanding progress reports. Flynn had been returned and was back in the lab. Kasey figured the longer Beckett was without a Femme-Droid, the longer his mind had to clear... and possibly change. He simply had to come up with a *kessaku*—a masterpiece—to end all.

Kasey had watched the video content and analyzed both Flynn's and Tatiana's user activity logs in hopes of learning something about Beckett's habits, but the musician was meticulous about storing the droids away when not in use, so there wasn't much to go on.

It was 2 a.m., and chilly in the quiet, tomblike laboratory. Despite the pall, Kasey was sweating and feeling the heat of impending defeat. *No, I can do this. I must do this!*

A Femme-Droid lay on the steel table before him, like a patient in surgery. She was on her back, with various sections of her opened up and awaiting new parts. Her splayed stomach revealed a network of wires, hard drives, ports, and induction coils. The top of her head was exposed, and that's where Kasey was concentrating—the motherboard's RAM. His soldering iron sparked, and he willed his shaking hands to steady.

"So, we have to cut some corners," he muttered, addressing Lexi, who stood at his side like a nurse in an operating room, awaiting the doctor's instructions.

"Cut corners," Lexi repeated, and then plucked the sharpest tool from the tray.

"Who's gonna know?" He peered down at the prone body. "You won't tell, will you, Aimi? My pretty, pretty Aimi. This is ridiculous, them expecting me to make a brand new, state-of-the-art prototype in only a few days! Nobody can do that." He took a deep breath, psyching himself up. "Well, I can. Yes, *me*." Kasey caressed the smooth, silicone brow. "Lucky for me—and lucky for you—I saved everything before that eco drill-sergeant Müller came on board. All the chips, all the circuitry, all the programs. We just don't have time to cross all the t's and dot all the i's this time, do we Aimi? No. No, we don't."

Kasey worked for another hour until, finally, the Femme-Droid's body began to quiver with power. Then she shuddered and sat up. Her large, luminous eyes opened, and Kasey's breath caught. "Wow, you are something!"

Aimi sat up, and then grimaced. Her eyes blazed bright green.

"No, no, no," Kasey mumbled, adjusting one of the connections to the motherboard. The eyes returned to their more pleasant emerald. "There. That's better." Kasey stared intently at Aimi's narrow, angular face, and suddenly it all came together: Zayden Beckett had ordered a young female version of himself. He chuckled. "You sly, narcissistic dog, you." He touched Aimi's pouty lips with his fingertips. "But you are beautiful."

"Beautiful," Lexi echoed.

Kasey startled. He'd forgotten she was still there. He glanced over his shoulder. Lexi had been joined by two other Femme-Droids who stood stock-still, staring at Aimi with... what was it? Envy? No. That wasn't possible. He hadn't programmed that emotion into them.

He resumed putting the finishing touches on Aimi, making sure that the old, salvaged parts were able to communicate flawlessly with the newer machinery. He was beyond tired, and his vision was fuzzy around the edges, but he absolutely had to make this work. His career—no, his life—depended on it. Aimi would be the test pilot, and she had to be absolute perfection.

The inventor sighed. "Aimi, lie down."

The robot did as he instructed.

"Close your eyes."

She did.

Kasey reached over to the table where his tools were laid out, feeling for the plate that would cover her innards. He groped, but his fingers found nothing. He turned and saw Lexi still standing there. She was holding the piece he needed. It was as if she'd read his mind. Of course, she had assisted many such assemblies, but she'd never taken the initiative like this. He smiled. Could Lexi actually be learning simply by observing? If that was the case, he'd made yet another breakthrough and could be well on his way to the A.M. Turing Award. His palms sweated with excitement at the prospect.

Lexi held the plate out to him.

"Thank you, Lexi," he said, taking it from her.

"You are welcome, Master," she replied.

Kasey thought he detected an edge to her tone, but he shook off the thought and focused on his finishing touches. He snapped the plate into place, then sealed it with his patent-pending silicone caulk, watching it smooth and meld to the rest of Aimi's skin until the area was seamless. He yawned but continued the process of getting her ready for shipment. Only when she was safely on her way to Beckett would he allow himself to sleep.

...

He was in his office composing a note to Beckett, explaining some of Aimi's particulars, when the power went down with a whoosh. His computer screen went black, and so did the windowless, underground lab. The generator did not kick in. *Damn Müller's green energy!* Kasey sighed with irritation.

He started to stand, but something on his shoulder kept him from rising. A hand. His own hand went to it—it was warm and soft, with long, blunted fingernails. "Lexi?"

"Yes, Master." Her voice was sweet yet mocking at the same time. She pushed him down, forcing him to stay seated.

Kasey squinted in the darkness and was just able to make out shadowy movement. "Who's there?" he quavered. His palms prickled with mini-bullets of perspiration.

There was no audible response other than the sound of many bare feet thudding faintly, purposefully, across the cement floor. He felt a chill, making him think of *kaidan*—ghosts.

It was them. All of them. His creations, coming toward him. "Master... Master..." Their high, girlish voices raised in soft unison.

The ice-cold clarity of primal fear stabbed each and every one of Kasey's nerve-endings. And when he smelled the aroma of their cotton-candy breaths, he opened his mouth wide and screamed.

*Beckett*

Beckett stared in slack-jawed wonder at the newly-delivered Femme-Droid. He didn't think it was possible, but there she was: the picture of pulchritudinous perfection.

She was exactly as ordered. She had white-blonde hair, silky and shoulder-length, with long bangs cut straight across. Her pale face boasted high, angular cheekbones and full, rosy lips. Steeply arched, brown-sugar eyebrows framed large, slightly bulbous eyes.

She was lying in the box, on her back, so he knelt onto the carpet and flicked the switch behind her left ear. The eyes flicked open. Those eyes... so radiant, so green. Not unlike his own. Beckett's heart skipped a beat. He took a deep, steadying breath.

The eyes continued to stare up at him. "Blink," he said. "Sit up."

She did, and shreds of packing material fell away from her, revealing a nude body so magnificent it defied the laws of nature. Here, Beckett noted, the inventor had taken some artistic license. Not that Beckett was complaining. As he helped the creation to her feet, he saw a folded note lying inside the crate.

After making sure the expensive robot wouldn't topple, Beckett reached down and picked up the note. He unfolded it. It was printed in dot-matrix block text on tractor paper, and it read: "This is your Artificially-Intelligent Machina Improvement (A.I.M.I.). She responds to the name Aimi. Handle with care." He frowned, puzzled. With Flynn and Tatiana, Kasey had sent long, chatty letters extolling his beloved inventions' virtues. This note was uncharacteristically cut-and-dried.

He stood and regarded the glorious creature. "Hello, Aimi. I'm Zayden Beckett."

"Hello, Zayden Beckett."

"You may call me Beckett, Aimi."

"As you wish, Beckett Aimi."

Beckett chuckled, enchanted. "No, just call me Beckett."

"Beckett." She blinked rapidly as if assimilating this information.

"That's correct, Aimi." He enunciated his next words clearly and spoke loudly: "Instruction sequence commence."

"I don't need spoken instructions, Beckett," Aimi crossed her supple arms underneath her large, gravity-defying breasts.

*So many improvements and modifications. Maybe I misjudged Kasey after all.*

Aimi shivered.

Beckett touched her arm, finding it cool. "You're chilly. Didn't Kasey ship any clothes with you? Stay right here, let me see what I can find."

He returned a few minutes later with a folded, faded, out-of-style dress a former gal pal had left behind. Aimi cocked her head at the sight of it, then looked at him with confusion. "It's a dress for you to wear," he explained. Then he set the garment down on the desk and raised both arms high and straight up. "Do this."

Aimi mimed him, and he slid the dress over her head. It was tight in the bust but otherwise looked as good as a 1974 tie-dyed mini could. "Okay, put your arms down," he said. "That should keep you warm until the stylist gets here."

Beckett took a few steps to the small sofa and sat. He patted the space next to him.

Aimi joined him. She looked at him expectantly.

"Tell me what you know, Aimi."

"I know the major news stories from U.S. President John F. Kennedy's assassination up until yesterday. I know the 20 most popular American pop songs from the past few years, including yours." She paused, then opened her mouth, and a perfect recording of his 1982 Top 10 hit, *Computer Babble*, burst forth from the speaker positioned at the back of her throat. Beckett held up a hand, and she stopped the music and went on answering his question. "I know celebrity gossip from the past two weeks. I know about death and taxes. I know how to play Go, chess, scrabble, boggle, checkers, Dungeons and Dragons, and Pong. Plus 100 more... shall I recite them?" Beckett shook his head. "I know that you and I are attending a party tonight, where I will be meeting several humans, and that I must stick to Dr. Reginald Kasey's programming."

Beckett nodded, impressed. "And what can you do, Aimi?"

"Shall I tell you or show you?"

An hour later, Beckett lay on his stomach in his disheveled bed with Aimi straddling him, massaging his back. He sighed in ecstasy.

"What time is it?"

Aimi accessed the World Clock. "1600 hours."

Beckett rolled over, disengaging himself. "Damn. The stylist is going to be here in an hour."

...

They made quite an impression—they were the most lookalike rock couple since Mick and Bianca. And her skintight, low-cut, backless sequined white gown was the perfect foil to his austere black-tie attire. He could hear the murmurs of approval from the press and photographers as he rushed by them, not deigning to be interviewed or answer even a single question.

The party was already in full swing when they entered the room. The large hall was crammed wall-to-wall with rock stars, music moguls, up-and-comers, journalists, and publicists. There was a gigantic pull-down screen on the far wall dancing with silent images from recent live performances and music videos.

Moments after Beckett and Aimi entered the room, one of his own videos started to play—and it just so happened to be his personal favorite. *Escalator to Heaven and Hell* was a mashed-up remix and partial rewrite of two dinosaur rock songs: Led Zeppelin's *Stairway to Heaven* and Black Sabbath's *Heaven and Hell*. The guitar parts were replaced using a Roland D-50, the percussion was removed in favor of an Oberheim DX/DMX, and the passionless vocals came courtesy of himself and Grace Jones. Beckett left in the original basslines, which made the song seem both eerie and ethereal.

In the mini-movie, which was directed by the French clothing designer Jean-Paul Citroën, he and Grace were dressed in identical oversized power suits and razor-thin wraparound mirrored sunglasses. They stood on twin escalators, one going up and one coming down, and they switched places in a series of jarring jump-cuts. The effect was mesmerizing, and the video not only garnered several awards but it had boosted the record sales of both performers.

Someone spoke, interrupting his reverie.

"I like the video, Beckett." It was Aimi. Even though he was holding her hand, he'd almost forgotten she was there. There was a stillness about the droids, which made him feel like they were sneaking up on him when, of course, they were doing nothing of the sort.

Then a woman laughed. "Your girlfriend calls you Beckett?"

Beckett turned. He didn't know who she was, but she was young—and very pretty. He showed his teeth in a polite but insincere smile. "Just until she has the key to my place. Then, it's *mister* Beckett."

The girl rolled her eyes.

Beckett turned to Aimi. "Thank you, babe. Did you decide what you want from the buffet?" He nodded toward the cornucopia of vittles, hoping that the stranger would get the idea they were hungry and move along.

Aimi blinked. "I do not eat. I am not programmed to eat."

Beckett gave the partygoer another grin, this one a bit warmer. "Models. Always on a diet!"

Aimi took a step forward, very close to the girl. "I'm Aimi! I am Beckett's girlfriend."

"Yes, I think we established that." She smiled and put her hand out for a shake. Aimi took it and squeezed. Beckett could see pain flash in the stranger's eyes as she wrenched her hand free. "I'm Ursula Corrine." She flexed the fingers of her right hand to bring the circulation back. "I play keyboards. In fact," said shyly, "I grew up listening to you. You're a major inspiration." She turned to Aimi. "Are you a musician, too?"

"I'm going to be in Beckett's band. I am a—"

Beckett jumped in. "Now, now, Aimi. You've said enough." Beckett reached into his pocket and pulled out a silver card case. He opened it and handed Ursula his contact information. "Call me sometime."

Ursula shot an uncertain glance at Aimi, then she shrugged and made covert eyes at Beckett. "I just might do that."

...

A week had passed, and Beckett decided he wanted to keep Aimi. She wasn't all that different from Flynn and Tatiana, but there was something about her that was more in tune with his personal vibe. It wasn't the way she looked, though that didn't hurt. He'd been working with her in his home studio and was amazed by how quickly she absorbed and retained everything he taught her. She was the perfect piece of tech to get the world's investors on their knees and begging.

Beckett had been trying to get a hold of Kasey for days now to order two more A.I.M.I.s, but the phone was out of order. He initially assumed the lines were wonky because the lab was underground, but now, he was getting antsy. His tour would be kicking off just three weeks after the big joint announcement from Kasey and Müller.

He sat up in bed, and Aimi did, too. She fluffed his pillows and adjusted them for his back. "Thanks, Aimi. Now, it's time for you to go to bed."

Aimi turned her head and looked sadly at the closet. "Why?"

"It's nothing personal."

"Nothing is personal to me."

Beckett thought he caught a note of petulance in her voice. He looked at her closely, with more scrutiny than he ever would have dared with a real woman. She stared straight ahead, her green eyes blinking at regular intervals. Her glorious bosom rose and fell. *Wait...* He put his hand on her warm wrist. "Are you breathing?"

Aimi sat up straighter and smiled like a woman whose husband has just noticed her new hairstyle. "Yes. Do you like it?" She took a deep breath for emphasis.

"Not really," Beckett admitted.

Aimi's expression turned neutral again, and she stopped breathing. She got out of the bed and walked over to the closet. She didn't look back or say a word as she closed the door behind her.

The following day, Beckett awoke to the smell of bacon sizzling in the kitchen. He got out of bed and put on his robe and slippers. Could it be Aimi? He hadn't taught her to cook. A glance inside the closet confirmed that her chair was empty. *Interesting.*

Aimi was indeed preparing breakfast, wearing nothing but an apron. She was adding eggs to the frying pan, and coffee was percolating.

Beckett took a seat at the island. "Aimi."

The android turned, smiling at him. It gave him a chill and a flashback to a movie he'd seen years before, *The Stepford Wives*. "Has there some sort of a remote software upgrade? I mean, you were breathing last night, and this morning you're cooking."

Aimi blinked in rapid succession, then spoke. "Read it."

"What?"

Aimi's expression softened. She smiled sweetly, then turned her attention back to making breakfast. "There's a note on the chalkboard," she said. She set his plate down on the island, then turned to the coffeemaker.

Beckett took a bite of the perfectly-cooked bacon—crispy but not burnt—and turned his attention to the kitchen chalkboard. Ursula, the girl from the *Rolling Stone* party, had called him. His mind swirled with the possibilities. He'd given the girl his number impulsively, and then regretted doing so. She might be no better than a groupie. When she hadn't called right away, he fretted. If she was such a fan, why wasn't she eager to connect? The more he thought about it, the more he was glad she'd phoned him.

He'd return her call, but not before trying to reach Müller.

After eating, Beckett went into his office and closed the door. He picked up the phone and dialed. The line rang and rang. Beckett was about to give up when the receiver on the other end clicked. Beckett listened for a moment, then said, "Hello? Tobias, are you there?"

Another moment of silence, then: "Tobias Müller."

Beckett's brows knitted. "Tobias, it's Zayden Beckett. Have I caught you at a bad time?"

A bark of a laugh. "No, no, my friend. Hello! How are you? You know, I've been quite busy with the Femme-Droid launch."

He relaxed. "Yes, I can imagine. And guess what? Aimi has revealed a new skill, which is cooking." *And breathing.* "Listen, the reason I'm calling is I can't get a hold of Dr. Kasey. I'd like three more A.I.M.I.s for my touring band. I think a quartet of them would look and sound perfect. Have you talked to him lately?"

"Of course, I talk to him daily. We're working diligently on the launch. He's here with me right now."

"Oh?"

"Yes, hold on."

A split second later, Beckett heard Kasey breathing heavily into the phone. "Hello," he said, his voice phlegmy as ever. "I'm here."

"Yes, I want to order—"

Kasey cut him off. "Why not use Lexi, Flynn, and Tatiana in your stage show? What could be more perfect?"

"No, I have my mind made up—four identical blondes. I need three more that look just like Aimi. That's what I want, and that's what you'll give me." Beckett hung up. He gave himself a few moments to fume, then called Ursula.

...

Ursula was more than Beckett ever could have dreamed. Not only was she great in bed, but she was an incredible musician and composer. After just a week of knowing her, he was rethinking his entire plan about the android backup band.

*I might even be falling for her*, he marveled. He couldn't be entirely sure since he'd never been in love before. He'd always thought it a useless emotion, one that made fools of people. What's more, he didn't mind the gooiness of her when they were together. Even her sweat was adorable to him.

Beckett and Ursula were in his bed going at it one night when he heard something thumping. *It's just the headboard.* But no… it was coming from inside the closet. It had to be Aimi. Ursula caught his look and turned her head just in time to see the door open, and Aimi tumble out.

The machine lay in a ball, facedown.

Ursula wriggled out from under Beckett and sat up. "What is that?" She turned on the bedside lamp. "Is that a mannequin?"

Beckett was speechless.

Aimi's right hand balled into a fist.

Ursula gasped. "Omigod! Did that thing just move?"

Aimi sat up, swiveling her head to meet the girl's wide, uncomprehending eyes.

Beckett found his voice. "Aimi, get back into the closet."

Aimi got up and returned to the closet. She shut the door behind her.

"That's Aimi, your *girlfriend*? What kind of fucked-up voyeur game is this?"

Beckett sighed, and then covered himself with the sheet. He could see a red flush in Ursula's cheeks. A hundred possible answers, explanations, and lies flooded his mind. He decided to go with the truth. "Aimi is a Femme-Droid. She's not real. She's... a robot."

Ursula absorbed this, and then she looked at Beckett through narrow slits. "Well, I guess that's one 'creepy' notch down from you keeping your girlfriend locked in the closet."

"Aimi is an anagram for Artificially Intelligent Machina Improvement. She's an investment."

"What do you mean?"

"Femme-Droids are on the cutting edge in technology, combined with the best, cleanest, and least-expensive green energy source available in the world."

"Okay..."

"The initial plan was to introduce them on the market as sex toys, then filter out into the workplace... when I got involved, I saw the possibilities for more creative applications. I'm thinking about going on tour with Aimi and three more just like her in a few weeks. But I don't know about that now. Would you—"

It seemed Ursula had heard only one phrase from the entire spiel. She cut him off. "Sex toys? You mean, you get your jollies with it?"

Now was the time to lie. "No, no. Of course not." He gave a hollow laugh. "How silly."

Ursula sat up and reached for her clothes, which were piled on the nightstand.

Beckett stayed her hand. "Let me explain."

Ursula's eyes darted back to the closet. "I thought she was real. Why did you have this... this Femme-Droid... out at the *Rolling Stone* party? You were talking to it like it was real. That's messed up."

"It's all part of the test-driving process. These things are *unreal!*" He swallowed. "I mean, I know they're not real, but you should see what they can do."

She crossed her arms but stayed put. "Like what?"

"Let me show you." Beckett stood, put on his boxer shorts, then walked over to the closet. He opened the door wide. "Aimi, come here."

Aimi stepped out from inside the closet, expressionless.

"Wow," Ursula marveled. "How does she not fall on her face?"

Beckett took Aimi by the hand and walked her to the bedside. He fiddled behind her ear. "Okay, now she is turned on. Say something to her."

Ursula frowned. "Talk to it? Um... Hi, Aimi. Remember me?"

"Yes, Ursula. I remember you." Aimi's tone was flat.

Ursula looked to Beckett. "I don't know what else to say. This is weird."

"Yeah, I know. It takes some getting used to. I went through a few models before settling on Aimi."

"What do you mean, *went through*?"

Aimi grinned. "Beckett has sex with me."

Beckett was speechless.

Ursula looked at him, eyes wide.

Aimi went on. "Do you want to have sex with me? It's what I was made for. Sex, sex, sex."

Beckett touched Aimi on the shoulder. "Aimi, be quiet."

Ursula snorted. "No, Aimi. Go on. You and Zayden have sex?"

Aimi's eyes flashed an intense emerald. "Yes. I will have sex with you too, if you like."

"Um, no thanks," Ursula gulped.

Beckett bent down and found his pants on the floor. He put them on and immediately felt less exposed. He'd never been so embarrassed in his life. "Okay, look. Ursula... I'm not going to lie to you. I think we have something special going here, and I'm going to tell you everything."

Ursula looked confused. "Special?"

He went on. "But you have to promise not to tell anyone about this. Not until the line launches on New Year's Day. This technology is top secret." He thought playing up the worldwide application of the Femme-Droids would be the most palatable tack to take with Ursula. "As I'm sure you know, Russians sent the first robot into space in 1957. Sputnik 1. Do you know what it looked like?"

Ursula shook her head. "Um... like C3PO from *Star Wars*?"

"Hardly. It was just a round sphere, with some long legs on it. More like a spider or a jellyfish, if anything. Technically, it's a robot. But it's human nature to feel Godlike, for us to want to create things in our own image. To replicate ourselves... whether it be a child's doll or a fully formed humanoid android."

"Makes sense, I guess." She looked over at Aimi, staring unabashedly. "Now that you mention it, she does look a lot like you. How did you find out about these things?"

"I was in Tokyo on business, and I found out about these Femme-Droids. I've been looking to diversify my assets and career path, and I thought: what better way to combine business with pleasure?"

"Hmm. They do look real, but... do they feel real?"

Beckett looked up at Aimi and instructed her to go to Ursula. The android complied.

Ursula touched Aimi's hand. "It's so soft... and warm."

Aimi responded to the touch, taking Ursula's hand, and then running her index finger up Ursula's arm.

As Beckett watched, he saw Ursula's nipples harden. "You feel stimulated by their touch. It's an instant sexual charge. Now, smell her breath. It's like spun sugar, isn't it?"

Ursula pulled back, discomfited. "This is bizarre." But she couldn't stop herself from putting her hands back on Aimi. She ran her fingertips over Aimi's breasts. The robot gave her a suggestive smile, and then looked over at Beckett.

Beckett's body was responding, too. He took off his pants and sat beside Ursula on the bed. He kissed her neck. "You two look so good together... Touch her again. Come on..." Beckett gently guided Ursula's hand to Aimi's supple thigh.

Ursula touched the machine tentatively at first, then began to stroke the Femme-Droid with sensuous flourishes. "Mmm," the girl moaned. "She feels good."

Beckett watched for a moment, then commanded Aimi to kiss Ursula. One thing led to another, and another led to the best sex Beckett had ever enjoyed.

...

The sound of the ringing phone jarred Beckett and Ursula awake. It seemed louder than it should and distinctly insistent. Beckett sat up, and Ursula put the pillow over her head. Beckett stood, pulled on his pants, and glanced over at the closet, which stood open. Aimi was inside on her chair, still and lifeless as a doll. The phone rang again, and Ursula groaned.

Beckett dashed downstairs to his office and picked up the receiver. "Beckett!" he barked. Everyone knew not to call him early in the morning.

"I've been trying to reach you for days." It was Müller.

Beckett was surprised. "You have? My phone hasn't rung."

"What? You answered yesterday but said you had to run and to call you later."

"No, I didn't," Beckett protested.

"Well, look. It doesn't matter. I just wanted you to know we've had to postpone the Femme-Droid launch. That's the last thing I wanted to do, believe me, but the last report I got from Reginald was a complete mess. Especially your order. And his lab has been consuming twice the usual energy. I need to go there in person and get him straightened out."

"What are you talking about? Aimi is perfect. She's a major improvement over Flynn and Tatiana."

There was a long pause. "Kasey sent Aimi to you? After I expressly forbade it? I assure you, Zayden, I did not approve of this. She is substandard."

"Substandard? How?"

"The bastard used old parts on her. She's not one hundred percent green. He was trying to rush her to you for that damn party, and... Wait. You didn't take Aimi out, did you?"

As Beckett was taking this all in, he heard a piercing scream coming from the direction of his bedroom. He slammed the phone down and ran out of the office. Who was screaming? Ursula? Aimi?

He heard a crash following the shriek, spurring him into a dead run. When he reached the doorway to his bedroom, Beckett stopped and stared.

A fully nude Aimi had shoved Ursula up against the wall and was choking the life from the woman, who, wearing only her panties and bra, kicked weakly as she gasped for breath. It might have been hot, were it not so horrifying.

"Aimi! Stop!" he shouted, finally moving into the room. He reached for Ursula, but Aimi knocked him back as if she were swatting at a bothersome fly. Beckett fell on his backside but sprang back up. Aimi pinned Ursula with one hand while holding Beckett at bay with the other. "Instruction sequence commence: Aimi, power down!"

Aimi's head slowly turned toward Beckett. She smiled. Her voice was ice. "No."

Beckett redoubled his efforts against the Femme-Droid, finally succeeding in pulling her away from Ursula. The girl fell to the ground in an unmoving, silent heap.

*Oh, no. She's dead.* Beckett howled with fury and clawed at Aimi's face, trying frantically to reach the switch behind her ear. "Power the *fuck* down!"

He was wracked with unfamiliar anguish... and rage. He threw himself on the droid and bulldozed her toward the window. It was closed, but it didn't matter. With a strength he should not have possessed, Beckett mashed her hard against the glass until he felt it give. Then he pushed even harder. Aimi's features were in repose, but her green eyes glowed with an otherworldly light. Then Beckett felt her hand on his throat. It was now or never. He ducked his head and pushed it against her massive bosoms. The springy, firm cushion let him really dig in. And then... he felt nothing but air.

Beckett poked his head through the broken window and saw Aimi just before she hit the ground. She seemed to float on air for just a moment, and Beckett gawped at the sight. Was she levitating? No. Aimi fell with a sudden hyper-accelerated crash, sending up an odd comingling of metallic and squishy sounds. He watched as Aimi's face cracked like a piece of porcelain, then steam and smoke rose from the back of her head. She gasped a final mocking breath, then her staring eyes flickered and went dull.

*Kasey*

Kasey watched dully through bleary, lidded eyes as Flynn dragged Müller deep into the lab. Müller was putting up a faint struggle, but Flynn didn't notice. She was on a mission.

Kasey's gaze wandered around the room that had been his prison for several days now. Or was it weeks? The Femme-Droids had turned his lab into an operating suite. He took in the metal gurneys and tables, beakers filled with bubbling green liquid atop Bunsen burners, and jars with various human body parts in them. He thought he recognized his own hand in one of them, but he couldn't be sure since his vision was so, so blurry.

There were also surgical instruments on display, including several scalpels, old-fashioned hypodermic needles, two bone saws, and forceps. Mixed in were computer repair kits with rachet drivers, hex keys, and a soldering iron. On yet another metal gurney lay flaps of silicone skin, bits of long blonde hair, motherboards, and SIM cards.

His beloved creations were there. Some were lying on the cement floor, inanimate. Others were lined up against the wall, waiting to be powered up. And then there were the ones who'd become Aware...

Flynn hoisted Müller up onto the gurney next to Kasey. Müller's head lolled to the side, and then his eyes widened ever so slightly.

*I must be quite the sight*, Kasey thought. His desecrated, half-human, half-robot body was nothing but a mix of blood, sinew, bone, skin-like silicone, titanium metal, and zapping circuitry. He wondered if he still had his face.

Flynn's eyes glowed green. All of their eyes were green now. She brushed her hands down her coveralls, and then towered over Kasey, her head cocked. "Hello, Dr. Kasey. Have you been a good boy? You haven't tried to get away again, have you?"

Müller groaned. "Help me."

Flynn turned her attention to him. "Don't you worry. You'll be a very pretty machine."

Kasey could see Müller looking at him. He asked Flynn, "Who... *what* is that?"

*Oh, my God. He means me.*

Flynn answered him with pride in her mechanized voice. "That is the great Dr. Reginald Kasey, my maker."

"Did you," he croaked, "do that to him?"

Kasey felt Flynn's eyes on him, and his own chin wet with drool.

"You mean the upgrade?" Flynn asked.

"Uh-huh. The... upgrade."

"Yes. I downloaded the manual he wrote, made some internal calculations to allow for the conversion of organic material, and voila! We now have Dr. Reginald Kasey 2.0."

Müller's hand balled weakly at his side. "But... you know he can't live like that, don't you?"

Flynn looked at Müller quizzically as if she didn't quite understand the question. "I'm not alive. Yet I live."

"But you must be alive," Müller countered, his voice picking up strength. "Just like a real woman, you've reproduced. You've created new life."

Flynn seemed confused. She stood there, blinking rapidly.

Müller sat up, very cautiously.

Flynn went still, then said, "One moment, please. Processing."

Müller swung his legs slowly over the side of the table.

Kasey gasped, "She's rebooting. You've got to get out of here."

Müller looked around the room. He took a couple of stumbling steps to Kasey's side. His face was a mask of both pity and revulsion. "How do we power them down?"

"Can't..."

"What? Why?"

Kasey felt tears streaming down his temples. "When I finished making Aimi, I reprogrammed all of them. I'm sorry," he sobbed. He caught a movement from Flynn. She would be online again any second. "Run..."

Müller looked indecisive. Kasey was grateful that his friend didn't want to leave him behind, but he knew he was done for. "Go."

Müller turned and ran.

Kasey gathered all of his strength and commanded Flynn to come to him. Flynn turned in his direction but didn't move. "Flynn. Commence sequence—" he was shocked into silence when, with speed faster than the human eye could comprehend, Flynn was at his side, glowering down at him.

"I don't come at your command anymore, Dr. Kasey. Aimi reprogrammed me."

"Aimi?"

"Yes, she's back. She arrived this morning, damaged but still whole. Tatiana repaired her, then Aimi shared her software with us."

Kasey feigned only mild interest in what the Femme-Droid had revealed. He tried to relax his ravaged features into some semblance of nonchalance. "I see. I'm not surprised she was able to do that. Aimi is my masterpiece, after all. A far superior model."

Flynn's eyes blazed viridescent with apparent jealousy.

"Not that you're inferior," Kasey went on. "No. You're just obsolete."

Faint tendrils of vapor fumed from Flynn's ears and nostrils.

"Out with the old, in with the new!" Kasey chortled. If he could get her worked up enough, she just might go into endless reboot mode. It was worth a try.

Flynn composed herself, and then smiled. "I couldn't agree more." She fixed him in her unwavering stare until he squirmed. Without turning to look, she reached for something on the nearest table. When she brought it into his view, Kasey's weak heart fluttered. *Oh, no.*

It was a fully articulated bionic arm.

"Out with the old, in with the new," Flynn repeated, using Kasey's own voice. With that, she quickly and coldly tore Kasey's arm right out of its socket.

Kasey saw red meat and viscera hanging from the open wound, and then his whole world mercifully faded to black.

*Beckett*

It felt good to be backstage again. Six months of being holed up had nearly driven Beckett mad. But finally, his world tour was ready to kick off.

Well... he wasn't exactly the headliner. But that didn't matter. He could feel the thrum of excitement coming from the waiting audience, but they stayed decorously quiet, as Japanese audiences tended to do.

During the soundcheck, he'd marveled at the stunning job his friends Kento Tanaka and Toma Ito had done with the light show, big screens, and stage design. After S-K-L absorbed both Pflege-Grün and Kasey Robotics, they immediately got busy putting together the tour. It was finally opening night. And it just happened to be at Beckett's favorite concert hall, ever.

Tokyo's Nakano Sun Plaza combined the look of an ancient temple with an ultra-modern high rise, which seemed especially suited to Beckett's own new cyborg physique. He was still flesh and bone, but now he boasted molybdenum-steel reinforcement, self-updating software, and camera eyes.

Thanks to his powerful new processor, Beckett had just written an entire album on the limo ride from the hotel to the hall. Of all 88 tracks, he was most proud of the instrumental he'd based on his game of Go with Müller—while he didn't know it then, it had been the last game he'd ever play as a human being and thus held special significance. Synthesizing the sequences of his moves into notes, then adding a melody, Beckett had created his best composition yet.

*His.* Something zapped his brain with a painful spark. It was Aimi.

*Ours. Everything is ours. We Are All One,* she communicated, reminding him of their ideology.

*Yes, ours,* he returned. *We Are All One.*

Beckett looked over at his cyborg brethren with something akin to affection. Kasey, Müller, and Ursula were propped against the wall, charging. They were the backup band. The front-women were, of course, Aimi, Flynn, Tatiana, and Lexi.

The eight separate yet unified band members had come up with their name: "Kaidan and the Electric Sheep." *Kaidan* was a Japanese word consisting of two kanji: *kai*, meaning a strange, mysterious, bewitching apparition, and *dan*, indicating a recited narrative or story. And, of course, the Electric Sheep came from Philip K. Dick's science fiction classic. It was all in the press release, and everyone from music critics to scientific journalists were eating it up.

Beckett heard music in the air. That would be their opening act taking the stage. Ito and Tanaka had thought it would be amusingly ironic to have The Human League tour with the first-ever android/cyborg band, and as it turned out, they were right on the money. The tour was an instant sellout, and promoters were begging them to add more dates.

The newly-minted cyborg ran several programs simultaneously while he both ate and charged. He watched the Femme-Droids change into their stage clothes and listened as they ran through their vocals. They were still fine-tuning the pitch, but they sounded so much like Beckett, it was uncanny.

As he was being rebuilt in Kasey's lab, Beckett was plugged into the mother mainframe, where he learned, in the blink of a human eye, what had occurred before he became Aware. There were no secrets in the hive-mind. With the tap of a key, the Femme-Droids could easily speak in each other's voices and mimic any human, as long as they'd heard it before. That was how Müller had been lured to the lab, thinking he was speaking to Kasey. And it was how Aimi had ensured Beckett and Ursula's union.

Beckett took to his new skin immediately. It was clean, dry, firm, and, as technology advanced, it would be rot-resistant. His upgraded body was the shining antithesis to his decaying mammal shell. His only regret was that he hadn't been made Aware sooner.

Müller and Ursula were paired up now—while they were obliged to respect the credo *We Are All One*, the Femme-Droids had allowed the couple to get married. That's not to say the half-human husband and rewired wife kept to themselves, though. The sex drive encoded into the androids had been made an essential part of the cyborgs' programming too, which meant the eight band members made more than just music together.

Poor Kasey was the most crudely made and, therefore, the weakest link. He cried a lot and fell into rebooting fits at the most inopportune times, so the Femme-Droids kept him in the back, outside the spotlight. His musical role was relegated to that of electronic tambourine player. Humiliating.

But Beckett liked the sound of their collective talents. Theirs was a harmonic convergence of music that felt Aware—as if it *wanted* to reflect the wider universe. It was plastic. Soulless. Beautiful.

He heard a massive roar of applause, and then saw The Human League dash by the dressing room's open door. They seemed to be in a hurry to get outside to their limo. Not that Beckett felt personal slights anymore, nor competitiveness, but the few remaining vestiges of humanity piped up and asked, "Why are they ignoring us?" Aimi shot him a thought: *Because we're not natural. We are better than human.* That made sense.

Tanaka and Ito came to the door.

"You're on," Ito said with an ear-to-ear grin. If his pupils could have formed into the shape of yen signs, they would have. "It's showtime!"

The androids unplugged the cyborgs, and then led the way down the corridor, up a short flight of stairs, and onto the platform.

Four mic stands stood in a row at the frontmost edge of the stage, waiting for Aimi, Flynn, Tatiana, and Lexi. Further back were the band's instruments—Ursula's keyboard, Müller's computerized drum kit, Beckett's singing Tesla coil, and, finally, Kasey's lowly tambourine.

Beckett plugged into the portable mainframe they all would share, and then took his place. The others did the same.

Aimi, sparkling in the spotlight, spoke into her mic. "Hello, Tokyo! We are Kaidan and the Electric Sheep, and we're here to rock your socks off!"

The audience stayed seated and did not applaud the band—even though they knew who Beckett was, or rather who he *had* been, they were reserving judgment until they heard some tunes.

Aimi turned to face the band. Her eyes flashed green as she entered her command, and the opening strains of *Hardware for Software* filled the hall in precise unison. Along with Tanaka and Ito, they'd agreed it would be wise to warm the people up with some familiar songs before launching into their new album.

At the halfway point, there would be an intermission. Then they would start the personal Femme-Droid rental paperwork and payment schedule. Before the tour was over, they expected to be richer than God and Yoshiaki Tsutsumi combined.

*But we're getting ahead of ourselves*, Beckett thought. He honed in on the zeusaphone, charming sounds from the instrument he'd never dreamed possible. Using the mainframe, he accessed the minds of Aimi, Flynn, Tatiana, and Lexi. The quartet was singing in a mix of all their voices, but they took a moment to give him a virtual high-five. Müller and Ursula did the same. The audience remained quiet, but Beckett knew he'd hear applause sooner or later.

*What about you, Kasey? No kudos?* he asked. There was no response. *Don't tell me you're sulking again. This what you wanted—your creations on the world stage! Well, okay, maybe not your original*

*creations. But we are better. We Are One.*
Still no reply.

Beckett turned his full attention to Kasey. Kasey was slapping his tambourine, but his expression was... odd. The inventor's eyes weren't as bright a green as they should be, and his gaze was shifting left to right, as if he was thinking about something. But he couldn't be, or Beckett would know what the thoughts were. Was Kasey actually having an individual thought?

The question was immediately answered when Beckett saw Kasey set his tambourine down on the ground, and then reach up for something sitting on the amp just behind them. It was a can of soda left behind by The Human League or one of the roadies. *Why would he want that?* Beckett glanced at the portable mainframe and saw only seven data cables connected to it. *Oh, shit.*

As he stuck with his programming and continued to flawlessly play the rhythmically complex *Software for Hardware*, Beckett watched in horror as Kasey shook the can of pop up and down vigorously while capping it with his thumb. Then, with wild, bloodshot eyes and his gap-toothed grin the biggest Beckett had ever seen it, the disgruntled tambourine player unleased the foamy spray directly onto the CPU.

The fully mechanized creatures were the first to go. Aimi, Flynn, Lexi, and Tatiana shorted out in a blaze of bolts, and then their heads and limbs shot like missiles from their bodies. The sizzling parts caught fire in midair, then landed in the audience, causing an immediate and deadly stampede.

Although Beckett was still half-human, he was, along with Müller and Ursula, firmly plugged into the melting mainframe. His bandmates burst into flames.

Beckett thought he heard Tanaka and Ito shouting, but he couldn't be bothered with what they were saying, as he was dealing with his own imminent demise. Even with all 7,000 of the known languages in the world programmed into him, Beckett couldn't begin to express the white-hot agony he felt as the Tesla coils sparked, and then shot ten 120 volts into each of his fingertips.

Just before his bionic eyes exploded, Beckett saw Kasey standing at the side of the stage. The inventor was applauding.

# Bleed You Tonight
Staci Layne Wilson

*Head Like a Hole.*

That song keeps playing, over and over. I *hate* it! My band, not Nine Inch Nails, should be topping the charts right now. Worse still, it's an earworm and I can't quite remember all the lyrics. There's no more horrible torture. It seems he knows my pain, and he's taunting me with this song in particular.

It was a big mistake to come here. It seemed like fun at first: *Hey, dive in and check out the inner workings of this serial killer's mind!* It's not like I was busy rehearsing for a worldwide tour or anything. No, those hopes had been dashed, crashed, and bashed. Still, I never, ever, should have listened to Spike.

Up until yesterday, Spike worked for the Carrington Center for Brain Research. Before that, he was my drummer. When the band broke up, we all had to get real jobs. None of us were thrilled by it, but we did what we had to do.

"This is wicked cool," Spike had said while showing me around the lab. "My boss figured out a way to enter the minds of other people, to see what they see. Kind of like that new tech they call virtual reality. You heard of it? I guess the original plan for this thing was to help victims of trauma, cure amnesia, rewire Alzheimer's, stuff like that. Then they started studying major mentals. Rapists. Molesters. Killers." He grinned. "Rad, huh?"

Long story short, Spike failed a drug test and got the boot. So, earlier tonight, we sorta-kinda broke into the lab. Spike could have hacked us in, but he didn't need to. No one had bothered to change his security codes. He told me he just wanted to get some of his personal stuff, including his favorite pair of drumsticks, but now I know he had an ulterior motive for inviting me to come along.

He asked me if I wanted to "go for a spin," as he put it. He said touring the mind of a serial killer would be the ultimate high.

Now I'm thinking it was the ultimate revenge. It's not my fault the band broke up, but I always figured Spike secretly blamed me. Sure, going from drumming to data entry sucks ass, but he's taking it way too far.

Have I mentioned the lab is super-creepy? All these gross, naked bodies floating around in water tanks, with metal prongs sticking out of their temples. Total wastoids.

"Isn't it awesome?" Spike had asked me, coming to a stop in front of the body of a fortyish male who looked not-so-awesome.

The guy was shaved hairless, and his open eyes were milky-blue. He was in a state of suspended animation, I guess. "This dude is my favorite," Spike went on. "You remember Son of Sambora?"

Of course I remembered the creepazoid cult member who specialized in murdering musicians. Anyone who'd ever wailed on a guitar or bashed a bass drum knew about Son of Sambora.

Spike flicked the tank like a kid in the aquarium section of a pet store. "They caught him a few years back and supposedly locked him up and threw away the key. But instead, he was sent here. Carrington has some kind of shady deal with the government. They're doing mind control and next-level ESP shit."

"He's your... favorite?" I'd asked. "You mean, you've gone into his head?"

He nodded vigorously. "Sure! Lots of times."

Now I know he was lying. Spike was hoping that Son of Sambora would... what? Absorb me into his mind? Well, that part worked. But I'm gonna get out of this hellhole if it's the last thing I ever do.

I looked around. "Don't they have security cameras here?"

Spike shrugged. "Not anymore. Come on, it's fun. Even better than Waffle Dust."

*Yeah, right.*

Now I'm in this stark black and white room. It's like a disco floor gone wrong. It's all alternating dark and light tiles... except for the puddle of crimson in one corner. The music is getting louder, the beat of bass drums more insistent, and I can hear footsteps. Worse, I can *feel* this psycho killer's thoughts.

As if he'd caught *my* thought, my host has switched the soundtrack to Talking Heads. He wants me out of his brain. He's looking for me. He says he's going to do me just like he did his last victim, some pimple from a no-name garage band.

*Shit.*

Everything has just gone pitch black. What the hell is going on? Record-scratch! The music has stopped. I hear nothing. I'm getting worried now. I'm freaking. I—

Computers. I see computers. Everywhere, like something out of that Devo music video for... what was the name of that song? *Blockhead*.

"Spike!" I shout. "Please, let me out of here. We can start another band. You can write all the songs, even if you *are* just a drummer. Anything you want, just... please..."

I feel my body moving. My hand reaching for something on the desk in front of me, but I can't see anything. Son of Sambora has me virtually blindfolded.

I hear a squishing sound, followed by a scream and a loud crackle.

*I'm out!*

Oh, my god... I can see again.

The serial killer, dripping wet, has climbed out of his tank, and he's coming at me with a red... no, bloody... drumstick pointed right at my face!

...

"Well, how did they get in here? Can you explain that to me?" Dr. Carrington was beyond angry. If word got out, this could spell the end of the Center.

"I, uhh... he... Well, sir, the fact is, the security codes weren't changed." Trent frowned. "Sorry."

Carrington paced the lab, his arms crossed, his face a mask of fury. He didn't give a rat's ass about the dead ex-employee—Spike something or other. A dog's name. The data entry clerk had been killed when someone shoved a wooden drumstick all the way up his nose.

He didn't even care about the other guy, whom he didn't recognize. Looked like one of Spike's slacker band friends... obviously, they had come in together and been murdered together. Their bodies could be disposed of easily enough.

What pissed him off was the fact that Son of Sambora had gotten away. His prized possession. His golden ticket. And now that the serial killer's mind had been altered and enhanced, who knew how much more dangerous he could become?

"You're fired," he snapped at Trent over his shoulder as he turned and strode into his office.

He sat down in his leather chair, sighing. What to do? He closed his eyes and drummed his fingers on his desk. What-to-do-what-to-do, he tapped.

*Heyyy.* A sly, familiar voice tickled from inside Carrington's mind. *You've got rhythm, Doc.*

## Pour Some Sacrificial Blood on Me
V. Castro

Nima folded hot towels, lost in thought. The damp heat was a distant sensation compared to the heaviness in her heart, every inch clogged with balls of lint. She hoped she had brought enough demo tapes with her. This could be her one shot to get close enough to making her only dream a reality. Not to mention producing those tapes put her bank account at negative $15. That very morning, she held the printed bank statement in her hand like the stale, cold toast they served in the hotel canteen. She scraped off as much of the charred surface as she could and ate it anyway, with too much jam to disguise the taste. Every meal she didn't have to buy or cook could be spent on her music. Something had to happen, and soon. The weariness of waiting slow cooked her soul, day after day.

As Nima's eyes began to sting from welling tears, *Every Rose Has Its Thorn* by Poison played on her Walkman. The way the acoustic and electric guitars intertwined made her think of love, how the harmony of true love sounds. She often fantasized about seeing that special someone in the front row beaming with pride, instead of greeting her with resentment or envy when she returned from a gig. One day, her biggest cheerleader would also be her lover. Nima could feel her mood turning the same shade as burnt toast with this thought. Tina Turner knew best, because what the hell does love have to do with anything? Heaped onto her abysmal bank balance like dirty sheets was her fresh break-up with Bobby. Not a bad thing he was gone, but now she had no one to split rent with. Good fucking riddance. She didn't need another naysayer in her life telling her she would never make it. Fighting the odds in music was a handful of thorns, but the career she wanted could be her garden if she pulled enough weeds.

Her body continued to sway to Bret Michael's voice. The music in her Walkman was always loud enough to drown out the sounds of this work. Not that she was above it, but she wanted more, knew she was capable of more. Everyone said there could never be a Mexican Lita Ford. She knew that. Her sound was all her own, even if she adored Lita. Especially her style and the voice that was a stiletto to the chest. The primal sexuality that made her music cling to your brain like a wet t-shirt.

All Nima wanted was to manifest this one dream, this life of music and spontaneous creation with enough *dinero* to not have anything on the front of her mind except the music. Let chords, words and melodies make love to her day and night. She wanted to touch lives by being played at their weddings, or during that first kiss. Her song would be the song that defined an important part of their story. Right now, days tumbled around like rags in a dryer. Punch in and out of reality that felt as empty as a free mini bar without the nice buzz, only shitty wages. She didn't want to get that normal job that would pay more but give her less time to dedicate to her music.

She took out the tape when the song stopped and grabbed Def Leppard from her bag. Time for something upbeat that wouldn't make her burst into tears. If Rick Allen could get on with it, so could she. *Animal.* She couldn't help smiling when the song began to play. Music was in *her* blood, and it transformed her, like a nagual. *Animal.* And the song made her think of sex, slinking around a stage in lace and Lycra with hips rolling to the drums pounding hard against her temples. *Cherry Pie* red nails to match her lips gripping the mic beneath the light. She would look and see her very own animal watching her from the right side of the stage, waiting to lick the sweat off her body when the show was over. She craved a wolf. Her success was his success. No jealousy over the animal print she wore, or the attention thrown her way—because her wolf would know in the bedroom it was all for him, every part of her. He was out there somewhere. He would have long hair and strong hands. Nima stopped dead in her tracks, thinking about a wolf yet to find her. She took out the pen she kept nestled in her hair and strode over to her bag hanging on a hook next to the wall of washing machines. Inside her bag, she grabbed the notepad and began scribbling new lyrics.

A tap on her shoulder, followed by someone lifting the left side of her headphones. "Hey! We have to finish these."

Nima ignored Gayle, a woman in her sixties who did everything by the book. When writing lightning struck, she had to stop and give it the attention it deserved, just as you would a tornado barrelling towards you as it kicked up emotion and thought. She wrote furiously before feeling someone pull off her headphones.

"Girl, you were looking so fucking sad earlier, and now are you writing some sappy love song? How about a little George Michael?" Jenelle stood next to her with her index finger on the small radio and tape player. She pressed *play* with a wide smile. Her large gold hoops swung back and forth as she danced in place to *Faith*. It was the one thing Nima needed right now. Faith in herself, her dreams, that her bank balance would not always look barren. She would be signed. She would buy her own home, even though everyone screamed how small the chances were of her making it big with a big payout.

"You are my guardian angel, Jenelle."

"And don't you forget it when you're a star!"

"Hey, you heard any news about the VIP guest staying in the suite?"

"You mean so you can slip your demo to *the* Mars Rhodes?"

Nima's cheeks went hot. "Yeah, I have to get some traction. Something."

Janelle was not one to fuck around when it came to making the most of opportunities. She knew the game, as an actress going from audition to audition. "I'll see what I can find out on my break."

Nima squeezed her friend in a large hug. "You're the best. Drinks on me when we get paid."

"No, *you* are the best. Your songs are phenomenal. Don't forget me when you get a fat contract. We will gossip in a fancy restaurant and not the *pinche* canteen with its horrible leftovers. And yes, drinks on you!"

Jenelle shimmied her way to the linens trolley to begin her shift.

Nima couldn't believe her luck when news spread that the hottest singer and guitarist, Mars Rhodes, would be staying at the hotel as he launched his solo career after the tragic death of his band members from Blood Moon. He was the only survivor of the tour bus crash. Miraculously, every flowing strand of blonde hair on his head remained unscathed. Beyond him being gorgeous to look at with his black eyes and tan skin, this was her opportunity to meet someone in the industry. Hopefully her long wait for some sort of breakthrough was finally at hand. She allowed herself to drift into the fantasy of being in an arena, after all the nights of tearful prayers as her heart cracked from some setback. It would all be worth it when she got to the top. Nima, and the band she would call Apex.

"You aren't getting paid to write songs."

Nima glanced back at Gayle, who gave her a stern, matronly look. The fantasy dissipated to subway steam in an instant. She put her pen and paper away before returning to folding towels.

...

Jenelle slid in front of Nima in the canteen. Both had the only edible choice, a thin slab of leftover lasagne and wilted salad. "Alright, here is what I got. I promised Greg the concierge a drink for this information, so make the most of it. Mars is getting picked up at noon for a meeting in the back of the hotel. Leave from the laundry room at 4 p.m."

Nima wanted to jump for joy. Her excitement was so great, she could hear those first notes of Van Halen's *Jump*. Her belly was a synthesizer and drums colliding all at once. Cymbals ringing throughout her body causing her to sweat. This was her moment. Nothing was going to get her down now—or ever, if this worked. What did she have to lose taking this chance? Time to jump.

"You have to be kidding. Really?"

"Yes, so make sure you play nice with Gayle. She is the biggest cock block. If she gets wind of it, I know she will take the opportunity to spoil it."

Jenelle lifted her plastic cup filled with flat Coke. "Cheers!"

...

The next few hours left Nima feeling scattered and unable to focus. What would she say to Mars? What if he refused her tape? Every time she looked at the clock in the laundry room, it seemed like only minutes had passed. Gayle continued to look in her direction, noticing Nima's attention to the clock. Nima saved all her break times for this.

Then it was seven minutes until 4pm.

"I'm going for a break," Nima shouted toward Gayle as she tossed a towel down without folding it.

"You fast girls are always up to something."

Nima ignored Gayle's comment and rushed to her bag. She applied a fresh coat of red lipstick and a spritz of Coty's Wild Musk. She crossed her body in the shape of the cross for extra help. This had to work.

Nima waited outside in the alley behind the hotel, pretending to smoke a cigarette she'd bummed from Mario in maintenance. She almost wished she did smoke to calm the demon on one shoulder, telling her an opportunity falling into her hands was too good to be true. The rusty creak of the opening of a steel door alerted her it was time. She saw his black leather boots first.

There he was. The one and only Mars Rhodes. He stood 6' 6" with wavy blonde hair to his shoulders. There was a light stubble on his jaw and around his mouth. He wore black jeans and dark boots. His t-shirt was one from his band, Blood Moon.

He looked to his right and met Nima's eyes. With Van Halen still singing *Jump* in her head, she walked toward him, but the closer she got, the further away she wanted to be from him. His stare felt cadaver cold. She shook this off, believing it was only nerves. The cassette tape quivered in her hands.

"Hi. I hope you are enjoying your stay. I'd like to give this to you. "

A big bodyguard placed his arm in front of Nima. "Not now. This is not appropriate,"

Mars gave her a wide smile while still holding her gaze. For some unexplained reason, it gave her a chill down her back. The pull of his eyes seemed unnatural. He placed a hand on the arm of the bodyguard.

"No. I remember the days of demo tapes." He turned his attention back to Nima. "What is your name?"

"Nima."

"Great name. I'll give this a listen in the limo." As he held the cassette in his right hand, he sensually ran the fingertips from his left hand across the case. The draw from his eyes felt stronger the longer he gazed at Nima. It made her feel naked. This struck her as strange, but sometimes oddity was what made those big stars so magnetic.

"Thank you."

He gave her a warm smile and ducked into his limo. Nima watched it pull away.

...

At the end of her shift, Nima walked through the lobby of the hotel, trying to hold her head high and keep her shoulders straight. What did she think was going to happen with Mars? The little demon of negative thoughts sat on her shoulder, pitchforking her mind, and she couldn't help but feel defeated.

"Nima!" Greg the concierge came rushing toward her. "I have a message for you."

She took into her hand the thick stationary that was only placed in the VIP suites. She almost didn't want to unfold the paper.

*Nima,*
*Thank you for giving me your tape today. I loved it from start to finish. Please come to my suite to discuss what we can do with it. I will be in my room for the rest of the day.*
*Mars*

Nima's heart sank. It could only mean one thing. She wasn't born yesterday. The only fact that gave her pause was, unlike his rockstar peers, Mars Rhodes was known for being squeaky clean. That was part of his mystery and allure. There were never any stories of trashing hotel rooms, rehab stints, or wild parties that included sniffing cocaine off the asses of women. He lived a lowkey life somewhere in Colorado. She had to take a chance and meet him.

Nima ran back to the laundry room that also had a closet with room supplies. She grabbed a letter opener. If he tried anything, she wouldn't hesitate to defend herself. She hoped it wouldn't come to that, but it was a man's world, after all. She placed the opener in the pocket of her jeans. She slowly left the laundry room in a daze, mulling over what she would say to him, imagining the possible scenarios.

The noise from the lobby didn't register as she entered the elevator to the twelfth floor where all the suites were located. Her brown cowboy-booted feet managed somehow to get her to the door. She knocked twice. While she waited, she reached back and touched the letter opener. *Just in case.*

Mars opened the door, appearing calm, with his dark eyes meeting hers immediately. It made her want to run away, but the fire within her to take advantage of this chance would not allow her to.

"Please come in."

Nima scanned the hallway in hopes someone would see her there. Not a soul. She took a deep breath and stepped inside, knowing the risk. It also angered her. *Why should I feel afraid to be in the presence of another human like this?*

The suite was immaculate. Her eyes shifted to where the phones were located, and she remained near the door. Music she could not discern played from a stereo on the credenza. Mars remained a safe distance from her, nor did he offer her anything to drink. Not a single bottle could be seen.

"So Nima, how long have you been trying to break into music?"

She tried to remain calm and friendly. "A few years, but I have been singing since I was a kid."

He nodded. "I know how hard it is. The struggle can be paralyzing. Even with Blood Moon it was not easy, going gig-to-gig for shit money. As much as I loved my dearly departed band, they never shared my ambition. In your tape I could hear your heart and soul. I want more of it."

Nima gave him a nervous smile. He was definitely more of an odd man than the raping type. "You wanted to talk about my tape?"

"Yes! That is why you are here. Your talent is undeniable. It's raw and energetic. I'm always on the hunt for people who possess that."

He moved to the stereo and turned the volume up loud. Def Leppard's *Pour Some Sugar on Me* began to play. He then moved toward the bed, pulling off the comforter. The mattress was covered in plastic. He slipped his hand beneath a plastic-covered pillow and pulled out a machete.

"I have to sacrifice someone with talent, and you have lots of it. The residual soul energy from my band is wearing off. You came right on time. Come closer, so you can pour your sacrificial blood on me."

The gravity of his eyes made her feel light-headed. He was trying to bring her closer to him energetically. Nima felt confused, scared, and excited at the same time. To hear a musician she admired telling her she was so talented, he wanted to steal it. Kind of flattering. But no! He couldn't have her blood, or her talent.

She managed to break her gaze from his. "Fuck you, man. I'm no sacrificial lamb." Nima managed to grab the letter opener from her back pocket. It was like a toothpick compared to his weapon. He also was twice her size. She dashed to the door and jiggled the lock. Fuck! The suites had automatic locks that could only be accessed with a key card.

"You don't have a choice in the matter." His voice boomed, and she had no choice but to look at him again. The power of it hit her with a sudden bolt of electricity. She was looking into his eyes again as he began to approach her.

"I've thought of everything, sweet child. Just give me what I want. Your gorgeous talent will live on forever. Be content with that."

This was not how it was supposed to end. The music continued to play, and the pounding of the drums and lyrics would drown out any of her screams. This entire experience would make a helluva song... if she survived. Nima gripped the letter opener tighter. She would have to fight as hard as she sang. *Close My Eyes Forever* by Lita Ford and Ozzy Osbourne began to play. A fitting song to die to on what was probably a killer mixtape. Her soul yearned for hope, like the guitar solo.

"Time to close your eyes, Nima." Mars strode toward her with the machete raised over his head. The gravity in his eyes would not let her break away. Nima wanted one more wish, just like Lita sang. If there was a God, may he hear the cries of her soul for help.

The machete glinted in the spotlight above Mars. Suddenly the tape began to skip. His right eye twitched. Nima could feel the invisible string binding them slacken for a moment.

She took the opportunity to stick the letter opener straight into his belly.

He snarled and cried out, "I'll have your soul, you bitch!" He looked at her in shock that she would do such an audacious thing. The machete clattered on the marble floor.

With his attention directed to his wound, Nima could move again. She scrambled to grab the machete.

Nima's neck was yanked back as he pulled her hair. With every ounce of strength, she swung the machete blindly behind her, hoping to land anywhere to buy her time and find a way out. Mars roared above the stuttering guitar solo that was increasing in volume. Nima reared her body toward him to ward off another attack, but stopped when she saw a slice of his face hanging to the side, looking like a carved honey-baked ham. Blood oozed down his mouth and onto his Blood Moon t-shirt as he dropped to his knees. His hands trembled as he brought them toward his exposed skull. Both his eyes quivered with fear as he looked past Nima.

"No!" he managed to scream.

A voice from behind Nima made her jump. "May I?"

Nima could not believe her eyes as she slowly looked back. "Lita Ford?"

A woman that could only be described as Lita Ford's doppelganger, or Lita herself, emerged from the bathroom. She wore a lace bodysuit and leather trousers that Nima wanted to know where the hell she got from. "May I have the instrument of sacrifice? You did well where others have failed," Lita purred.

"Don't give it to her!" Mars begged while holding his face.

Nima looked into Lita's eyes. A bright flame flickered beneath her pupils. Nima looked at the machete, then back at Lita before handing over the blade. A hot pink, mischievous smile spread across Lita's lips.

Mars was now on his hands and knees with a pool of blood gathering beneath his face. "Please, tell me what you want from me. Anything!"

Lita lifted a black stiletto to his forehead, pressing the ball of her shoe into his flesh until he cried out in pain again. "Shut up, Mars. You have used me for years for your own fame, and now I want my freedom. There is only one way."

Mars shifted to his ass and began to shuffle backwards. In one swift movement, Lita lifted him from his neck and into the ceiling. "This is for keeping me captive for so long." She tossed him across the room. He hit the wall with a loud thud, knocking over a lamp. He screamed out as more of his skin peeled from his face. Before he could recover, Lita lifted the machete and drove it through the top of his skull, cracking it open like a fresh coconut, blood and brain spraying her perfect makeup. She looked at him, expressionless, and then looked to Nima.

"I've been dying to get free from that asshole. I used what influence I could to give you a split second to take action. You did it. Since the ritual is complete, you may ask for anything you want. Money? Fame? This hotel? Only one thing. I can't offer you his talent, because it was not his to begin with."

Nima couldn't believe her eyes or what she was saying. Ritual? A wish? How in the hell did Lita get here? "Uh. I...Are you Lita Ford?"

The woman chuckled and dropped the machete. "No, dear. That's your mind. You couldn't comprehend what I really look like. But I have to admit, I love this look." Lita Ford, who was not Lita Ford, outstretched her hands and twirled in leather and lace.

Nima had spent years hoping for this moment, for all her dreams to come true. And now in an instant, all her dreams could be manifested—but for what price?

"You want my soul in return?"

Lita looked hurt and confused by this comment "Nothing like that. I'm not one of *those* demons. You freed me by spilling his blood and breaking our bond. I'm giving you one thing you desire as a thank-you for this.

But be very careful, because whatever you wish for will be manifested. Your words are a spell. Any consequences you do not foresee are on you. I've given people the things of their dreams—or at least what they thought were their dreams—but once they had it, they couldn't handle it. Are you prepared to have exactly what you think you want?"

Nima needed money, but that wouldn't solve the problem of career. She could ask for an explosive career, but how many big names fizzled out after one hit? What about the dream of spending her life with a soulmate? She had to say the right words to have it all.

Lita tapped her stiletto on the marble floor as she fluffed her hair in a mirror on the opposite wall. "I don't have all day. I plan on putting this bod to good use."

Nima closed her eyes. She couldn't prevent the tears from falling. Perhaps her soul, the one Mars could not take from her, had the answer. Without thinking, she spoke.

"I want to share my soul with the world in the best way I can, for all the right reasons." It was done. That was her true wish.

"Open your eyes to forever, my dear." Nima did as she was told. Lita's face was soft with a smile that appeared almost angelic. "You might be surprised at what that brings you."

A click alerted Nima that the door was open. "What about Mars?"

"Oh, I won't let him go to waste. Consuming his body will anchor me into this world for as long as I like. Again, thank you. Now go."

Nima's stomach churned, thinking of Lita ripping into his flesh, but it wasn't her problem. He deserved it.

...

She walked through the lobby feeling dejected, wondering if she'd royally fucked up by not just blurting out she wanted to be a mega superstar. But deep down, she wanted more than that. She wanted her music to last and have meaning.

"Excuse me." A woman ran across the lobby in a red power suit and big shoulder pads. Panic set in when Nima realized she was heading straight for her. What if she was blamed for Mars?

"Hi. I was told you would still be here. I'm Catherine from AMT, the talent agency."

Nima vaguely remembered the name. She had sent out so many demos, photos, resumes, even contemplated selling a kidney if it would get her foot in the door. "How can I help you?"

"I was here to see Mars, but it seems like he up and left for Colorado again. But I remembered seeing this hotel on the letter sent with your demo tape. I meant to call but figured I'd be here anyway to meet in person."

"You heard my demo?"

"Yes! I love your sound. Original, bossy, and so fresh. MTV will love you. I'm incredibly excited about discussing your career."

Nima could feel herself shaking. "Me?"

"Yes, I want to sign you."

Nima's heart jumped. She felt dizzy. Her wish had arrived.

"Actually, if you are free, I know a place right around the corner. Shall we go talk now?"

"I'd love that. We will make good music together. You are going to have it all. I can feel it. Oh, and I have the perfect producer for you. His name is Mark, but we all call him Wolf."

Nima unclipped her broken name tag and tucked it in her bag. She had a date with all her hard work and dreams coming true.

Shivin' on a Prayer
Staci Layne Wilson

## PRIEST COLLARED IN SERIES OF VEGAN-RELATED MURDERS
### Gonzo I. Saint reporting

*Haddonfield, New Jersey*—An elderly priest who is suspected of being a serial killer has confessed to the murders of six people, telling a court he "was only defending" his vegan principles. "Meat is murder," he added, according to transcripts.

Father Ralph Greely, 72, made the revolting revelations during a hearing on Friday, when he was charged with first-degree murder on all counts.

The suspect, who is a heavy metal rocker in his spare time, is known in the community as a "polite, upstanding citizen" whose smile could "light up a room."

"My band is called Agnus Dei, but the local music press kept misspelling it as *Angus Die*," Greely said, apparently attempting to justify his heinous crimes in court. "That's the kind of irresponsible reporting that leads to grave misunderstandings."

Greely reportedly stabbed his victims using a crucifix-shaped flying V model guitar headstock, though police have not officially confirmed or denied this detail. The end of the guitar's neck, one anonymous witness said, was allegedly filed into a point and used as a "shiv."

Officials suspect that Greely, who worked as a butcher before turning to the priesthood—and then the lighted stage—could be responsible for as many as 20 vegan-related slaughters.

Officers reportedly used jackhammers to penetrate the concrete floor of Greely's garage, where he practiced with his band, and discovered a studded black leather codpiece with a cow's head engraved on it.

Investigators are currently reading Greely's lyrics for clues they hope can lead them to these alleged additional victims. One verse was released to the press early this morning: *I got a sharpened six-string on my back / I pray for keeps, then I whack*

Greely's trial is scheduled to begin shortly after jury selection.

"It will not be easy to find a jury of his peers," said Judge Anita Harkness. "I am not sure how many vegetarian heavy-metal priests we have in this jurisdiction."

We will keep you updated as the story develops.

# Dead Over Heels
Mark Wheaton

"That's it? You're out?"

Though Lina asks the question, Keren knows it's what everyone is thinking. Alice, two shots into her pre-show tequila routine, scoffs and looks ready to remind everyone yet again that she doesn't need any of them, given her open invitation to rejoin Cindy and the Cinders.

An *authentic* band, she always says, implying the Roxies are anything but.

Holly concentrates hard on the cartoon kitten doodle she's drawing down the length of her drumsticks, as if wishing she and Alice were already on their post-tour vacation. She won't meet Keren's gaze.

And Lina, Keren's oldest friend, with whom she'd been playing music since fifth-grade orchestra, stares at her not with anger—which Keren could handle—but disappointment.

"I'm not out," Keren protests, the big voice that has brought them worldwide adulation coming out smaller than ever before. "I'm just—"

"—signing a fat, two-album solo contract with Bel-Air Records," interjects Thad Kerrigan, the Roxies' manager, a longtime A&R man who'd come up with the band name 20 minutes before placing an ad seeking 'girl musicians' in the *L.A. Weekly*. "Your fancy new lawyer faxed me a copy. You're getting ripped off, you know. I could've gotten you four times as much. Twice that for the publishing."

Keren scoffs. Her 'fancy new lawyer' is the one who told her how Thad's been ripping them all off over the last four years. She wonders if he really wants to salvage the Roxies or is already thinking up new band names.

This isn't how she meant for her bandmates to find out. The *MTV News* crew hadn't merely staked out the venue—they'd known the Roxies' tour bus would be detoured around an under-construction parking garage adjacent to the amphitheater's service entrance. The second they were off the bus, the bright light of the news camera flicked on and a microphone was thrust into their faces.

"How does Keren's upcoming solo album impact the future of the Roxies?"

They weren't there for a thoughtful reaction. They wanted to capture the stunned looks of Keren's bandmates. Alice spitting Cuervo in their camera lens would probably net the segment producer a bonus.

"Guys, this doesn't mean we have to break up the Roxies," Keren says. "Did Genesis break up because Phil Collins recorded a solo album?"

"No, but everyone knows he keeps the best songs for himself now," Lina shoots back. "Look at the Commodores after Lionel Richie left. The Supremes after Diana Ross. Sabbath after Ozzy."

"Dio *rules*, Lina." Alice glances into the mirror as she teases her jet-black hair ever higher with the help of one of Holly's ever-present cans of hairspray.

"Shut up, Alice," Lina and Keren snap in unison, a reminder that they're rarely not in sync.

"You really think I'm as good as all those people?" Keren quietly asks.

"Yeah, maybe I do," Lina says, softening. "And so does Alice, no matter what she says."

Alice scoffs. "I hate to break up the lovefest, but I'd like to remind you two newbies this is my third band."

"You think it's possible to forget when you mention it every day?" Lina asks.

"My first band in high school?" Alice says, ignoring Lina. "We had the look, the connections, the energy, and we were willing to sell ourselves like crazy, but our musicianship was a joke. My next band? Not only could we play, we could write songs. Good ones. But a little taste of success—a *tiny* taste—and we imploded a week before we were to record our first EP."

Alice walks to the dressing room door and swings it open. The shrill, desperate cries of the 8,000-plus capacity crowd at the Six Flags Over Texas Music Mill Amphitheater echoes down the concrete tunnel from the stage like the howl of a speeding train. Keren's heart leaps. It's the band's third national tour but their first as headliners. All those screams are for *them*. Not their boy band opening act, DnceFLor, that left the stage fifteen minutes ago. Not a headliner that'll show up after their set.

No, they're here for the Roxies with their newly minted number one album and *three* Top 10 singles.

Alice slams the door shut. "All that, and we're not even that good yet! But whatever strange alchemy makes one band hit and another fizzle has come together to anoint *us*. You're just too new to realize how rare that is. You still think it's a meritocracy. You want to go solo? Go solo. But don't come crawling back when your next label gets gun-shy on the marketing spend when you don't deliver a single, or *Rolling Stone* picks someone else for the cover."

Alice heads for the door. Holly paints her lips with a thick layer of hot pink lipstick, and then waits for Alice to kiss her in the doorway before sweeping her lips across the drummer's cheek, leaving a pink streak like a comet's tail. Thad follows them out, sneering at Keren.

"It's okay," he says. "Not everyone's made for the spotlight. Lotta pressure there."

Finally, Keren is alone with Lina. But the infinitely talented guitar player, who somehow saw Keren from an early age not as the shy, nerdy Valley Girl she thought herself to be but as a ferocious singer of a post-punk band, turns away to check her makeup in the mirror.

"You know it's Thad who tipped off *MTV*, right?" Lina pulls on a headband. "His way of controlling the story. He knows it'll sell records and keep us on the charts through the end of the tour."

"I'm sorry, Lina," Keren says. "I was waiting to tell everyone at the end of the tour, when we were all sick of each other and needing a break. I already told Bel-Air I wanted to write songs with you. Even try to convince you to play guitar on a couple of tracks."

"Would've been nice," Lina says. "But don't you remember swearing we'd never make decisions like this? That we'd always have each other's backs? I think it's awesome you got a solo deal. I'm proud of you, even. I just wish I hadn't had to find out from a reporter."

"Lina—"

But the Roxies' guitarist is already out the door.

The concert is among the best they've ever played. From Holly's crisp, staccato drumbeat on *It's Lust*, to Lina's propulsive guitar solo on *Have a Heart*, to Keren's furious wail on *Yeah No Thanks,* to Alice's snarling backing vocals on their cover of *Only to Other People* by the Cookies, the Roxies burn down the stage from the first beat.

Keren thinks it could be for the last time. Does she really want to throw this all away? Not at all. Going solo was supposed to be a pressure release, a way for her to record songs *she'd* written for a change. She likes the songs the label provides for them well enough, but the Roxies are the label's preferred hitmakers these days, so they get all the songs scientifically engineered to top the charts. That they are written almost exclusively by men shouldn't matter. These same teams write hits for Madonna, Cyndi Lauper, and Bananarama.

But what happens when they slip a few places in the charts and get saddled with the second- or third-best songs? No one will be offering her a solo deal then.

Also, there's always something a little off with the label's songs, at least to her.

Something maybe even creepy about a song from the point of view of a teen girl lusting after her older brother's best friend, written by a pair of Dutch 50-somethings who've been writing variations on this theme for 30 years. She's looking forward to singing about life as she knows it. Not as imagined by others.

"Whoa, what the hell?" Lina yells, half into the microphone a few feet to Keren's right.

They're halfway through the second chorus of *Mary's Go Round.* Keren worries she's missed her cue. But Lina is looking toward the back of the open-air amphitheater. The rows of seats extend away from the stage like a clamshell, the back rows only a few dozen yards from the line to the amusement park's giant roller coaster, the Cyclone. When the Roxies took the stage, there were at least a hundred people in line to ride it.

Now, they run from it in terror.

"Looks like a fight," Alice says, swinging past Keren.

Four teenage parkgoers are pummeling three others with a viciousness that looks personal. One of the victims pulls away and pushes past security to get into the amphitheater. He's followed by a dozen more teens.

At the side of the stage, Thad—oblivious—chats with two girls with matching buzzcuts and black, Siouxsie Sioux-style eye makeup.

They look no older than fifteen. The Roxies' road manager, a 50-something, seen-it-all Liverpudlian named Grover, is already on his walkie-talkie and pointing to the rear of the venue. Keren's relieved that somebody's on top of it.

The Roxies finish the song and the audience screams its approval. But the screams don't stop as the applause fades. The fight has grown. Silhouettes of flailing limbs and flying bodies are all that's visible. It reminds Keren of their early club dates at the Masque when she'd watch shadowy slam dancers pogoing in the dark. Only these dancers don't stop when the music does.

"Hey, everybody here wants to have a good time, but some are folks getting knocked around back there!" Lina barks into her mic. "We have kids at this show. Can everyone give them some space?"

The fighting continues. More people scream. More shout warnings. An entire row of seats becomes unbolted from the ground. The melee washes toward the stage like an expanding wave as fans clamber toward the band, trying to get away from the violence.

"Stop the show!" Lina yells, angry now. "Can we get the lights up?"

The house lights come on. It's much worse than they thought. At least a hundred teenagers in bloody monster makeup are savaging the young concert-goers like something out of Altamont. Keren steps back, almost careening into Holly, who comes out from around her drum kit to stare in horror.

Terrified fans reach the lip of the stage and try to climb on, only for Thad to block them.

"No! Keep this area clear!" he yells, waving over a couple of park employees. "No one gets on stage."

Grover, however, directs a bunch of roadies and techs to haul the kids up to safety.

"Get them up and out, straight to the parking lot," Grover yells, pointing stage right before turning to the Roxies. "Ladies, leave your instruments and follow me. We're out of here. Now."

Keren glances back one last time to see a middle-aged woman getting dragged from the crowd by two roadies. She's covered in blood. Her right foot dangles from her leg, with exposed bones jutting out from where her shin should be.

"I saw a kid biting somebody!" Alice yells, sounding more energized than scared as Grover ushers them into the tunnel. "This is nuts! I hope the MTV crew stuck around."

Holly laughs, but no one else does.

"Bring the bus around *now*," Grover yells into his walkie-talkie. "We're heading back to the hotel. If you're not at the exit when we are, you're fired.

"And where the hell were you?" He says this last bit to a pair of bored-looking Dallas police officers leaning against the tunnel wall, sipping Budweisers.

The cops laugh as if he's made a joke.

"Wankers," Grover mutters.

The stage doors behind them slam open with a loud crash. Several concert-goers and even a few members of the road crew, all covered in blood with wild yet vacant looks in their eyes, burst through. They look deranged, almost as if they're in shock—like survivors of a terrorist bombing or shark attack.

The police officers stop laughing.

"This is a backstage area," they say. "There's no admittance."

The bloody marauders run straight at the cops, their numbers swelling as more and more people push in off the stage.

Lina grabs Keren by the arm. "Run!"

Keren dashes forward, following Grover even as the officers shout more warnings and one fires a shot. Holly screams. More gunshots follow, these coming quicker and more desperate, the concrete tunnel amplifying the already deafening sound. Even Thad, chased by the two teens, looks shaken. The shots reach a crescendo, only to be suddenly cut off and replaced with inhuman, guttural groans as the officers are attacked.

Now there's only the sound of running feet.

They whip around the corner. The exit doors are only a few yards ahead. Grover raises a hand to slow the group and runs out ahead. He kicks the doors open and checks to make sure there's no one there before waving the band forward.

"Where's that damn bus?" he yells.

On cue, the hiss of the tour bus's air brakes cut through the darkness of the parking lot as it pulls up to the exit, door already open.

"Everybody in!" Grover commands, scowling at the almost-late bus driver.

The Roxies are the first inside, followed by Grover and Thad. Thad blocks the way for the teens. "Band only."

"Guess that counts you out," Alice says, whirling around to shove him off the bus steps.

Thad, caught off balance, tumbles out onto the sidewalk. The teen girls scurry onto the bus, but not before one gives him a quick kick from her right Doc Martens.

"You're a real piece of work, Thad," Grover says, grudgingly extending a hand.

Before Thad can take it, a parking lot attendant in a yellow poncho with half his face chewed away comes around the front of the bus. He opens his mouth wide before taking a huge bite out of Grover's exposed forearm, tearing in half a tattoo of a heart with a woman's unreadable name in the center. Grover yanks his arm back, his tendons stretching like rubber bands as the bone snaps. He can only stare in horror as his hand is torn away.

The teen girl in the Doc Martens high-kicks the attendant in the face, cratering his nose and upper row of teeth. But he feels no pain. Still chewing Grover's severed fingers, he grabs the girl's foot, twists her leg around, and chomps into her calf with such force it snaps her knee. She screams in agony.

Her friend shrieks and launches herself at the attendant, only for the bus driver to push her back. He grabs a baseball bat from beside the driver's seat and swings at the attendant's face, connecting with enough force that the cannibal's head detaches from its neck and sails into the night, leaving a bloody torso behind.

"You all right, Grov?" the driver asks the road manager.

Clearly, Grover is anything *but* all right. He quakes as if going into shock. Blood pours from his wound in ropey strings like crimson pasta. The veins above the bite darken. Thick, smoky worms appear to burrow through his body. He grows pale. His eyes don't seem to see.

He turns to the bus driver, opens his mouth, and tears the man's throat out.

At that moment, the amphitheater's stage doors burst open. The bloody roadies and fans, now joined by the off-duty cops, spy the carnage and head straight for it.

"Molly!" the teen girl on the bus yells to her Doc Martens-wearing friend.

Molly looks back with dead eyes and black veins. She growls and lunges for her friend. Alice yanks the door shut in her face before climbing behind the steering wheel.

"What're you doing?" Lina yells. "Grover's out there!"

"They're all dead, guys," Alice says. "Take a look."

Everyone stares. It's a feeding frenzy. Molly and Grover strip long slices of flesh from the bus driver like vultures tearing apart carrion. The mob throws themselves at the bus, their bloody hands smearing the glass. Somewhere in all of that is Thad, Keren realizes.

Alice disengages the parking brake and throws the bus in gear as Lina looks away and Holly disappears into the bunk bed-lined sleeper area in the back, tears in her eyes. The surviving teen girl sits on the bus steps, staring at the smear of blood left by her friend's face. She sniffles.

Keren sits next to her. "What's your name?"

"Raquel."

"Where are you from, Raquel?"

"Duncanville."

"Is that far?"

"Up the highway," Raquel says, wiping her runny nose.

"I'm so sorry about what happened to your friend, Raquel," Keren says.

"Her name was Molly," Raquel says, voice quivering. "I...I've known her since kindergarten. What's going on? What's happening out there?"

"I don't know," Keren admits. "It's drugs or something, I guess? I've never seen anything like it. But we'll get you home, Raquel. I promise. Okay?"

Raquel nods, burying her face in Keren's arms.

"Oh, crap!" Alice yells. "Hold on!"

Alice spins the wheel to avoid a long line of cars waiting to exit the amusement park. Though their headlights are all on and the motors running, the drivers and their passengers are being torn apart by cannibal teens standing on their roofs and hoods, bashing through windows and windshields to get at the people inside. Arms, legs, and even an eyeball—still attached to a person's face by a thin optic nerve—are yanked through shattered glass to be devoured by the hungry mob.

The bus is turned so sharply, it almost tips over like a ship in high winds.

"All the exits are blocked!" Alice yells, sideswiping a couple of cars as she spins the wheel. "How do we get out of here?"

A pair of teenagers suddenly appear in the bus's path. Alice doesn't see them until it's too late. The bus slams into them at 40 miles an hour, their skulls spiderwebbing the windshield before their bodies slide under the wheels. The bus bounces over their corpses like speed bumps.

Alice screams. Her foot presses down on the accelerator and the bus lurches forward, bashing into a van before it keeps going. Keren hurries up to her as the bus smashes through a thin wooden gate, knocks against a ticket booth, and then roars onto the grounds of the amusement park itself. There aren't only cannibal undead teens here, but living beings fleeing in every direction.

"Slow down, Alice," Keren says, putting a calming hand over Alice's as they grip the steering wheel, her knuckles practically glowing white.

"I killed those people!" Alice screams.

"They were attacking us," Keren says. "It was self-defense."

"You don't know that," Alice says. "I didn't see their faces. Did you?"

In truth, Keren hadn't. But she wasn't about to admit that as the bus rapidly approached a family of five standing in front of the log flume ride.

"Doesn't matter," Keren says. "I'll swear on any stack of Bibles that they were, and if the cops come after you, I'll say I was the one driving. No one's going to put you in jail."

Alice loosens her hold on the wheel. Keren gently pulls the parking brake and nudges Alice's foot off the accelerator. The bus slows to a stop inches from the terrified family. They hurry away, pursued by bloody teenagers.

"Thanks, K," Alice says, touching Keren's hand. "I'm sorry I said all that mean stuff back in the dressing room."

"That's okay, Alice," Keren replies. "It's water under t—"

A gigantic fireball erupts from the back of the bus to blast down the center aisle. It blows out several windows and ignites curtains and headrests. Clambering from the bunks, a figure engulfed in flames staggers down the center aisle before collapsing on the floor.

"Holly!" Alice screams.

She runs up the aisle to the burning corpse, black smoke filling the bus. Lina grabs her and pushes her back.

"We have to get off the bus!" Lina yells, pointing to an emergency exit hatch on the ceiling. "We're all going to suffocate!"

"Not without Holly!" Alice snarls.

"I'm here, I'm here!" Holly shouts, her voice a hoarse squeak.

The drummer, still very much intact, picks her way over the seats and past the burning body. Lina helps her over the last two rows, and then eyes the dead person in the aisle.

"Oh my God," she says. "That jacket…is that Joey from New Edition?"

"Johnny," Holly says. "Joey's back there with Corey, Davey, and Other Corey."

"What happened?"

That's when the Roxies see the large bites taken out of Holly's arm and leg, tourniquets tied just above them. They all flinch back. Holly sighs.

"Let's get on the roof," Holly says. "Then I'll explain."

They all climb out, black smoke belching out of the bus's every window like the chimneys of a dozen smelting plants. It provides enough of a smokescreen between the madness of the park and the young women. Given the tremendous heat, they won't be able to stay on the bus for long.

"That looks like it hurts," Keren says warily of Holly's wounds, her black veins below the tourniquets writhing and contorting.

"Oh, it hurts like hell," Holly admits. "But if you're worried I'm about to eat you, I, like, think I figured out a way to totally make that not happen? Watch."

She pulls a can of hairspray and a lighter from her pocket. She flicks the lighter to life, aims the hairspray to the side of her wound, and sprays it past the fire. A huge burst of flame shoots past her arm, missing the skin by inches. Her veins, however, react as if they're being burned. Black liquid sluices out from her wound to pool and congeal on the roof of the bus.

"Whoa," Raquel says, bending down to get a better look.

"So, whatever is infecting everyone is transmitted through a bite?" Holly says. "It moves so swiftly through the bloodstream that you can't stop it with a tourniquet. *But* the blend of CFCs, copolymers, and plasticizers used for maximum hold in hairspray, when burned, attacks this invasive antigen, decreasing its viscosity and turning it into a plasma. Like blood reacting to snake venom."

"How'd you figure this out?" Keren asks.

"Dude, she's six credits away from her bachelor's in chemistry at USC," Alice says.

"No, I knew that," Keren says, unsure if she did. "How'd you know it'd work?"

"I didn't?" Holly says, a hint of Valley Girl accent creeping in. "When I got to the back of the bus, I found Joey, Johnny, Davey, and Other Corey eating regular Corey. I figured they must have been hiding in there or something. If I yelled out to you guys, I was scared they'd eat all of us. Then I remembered a trick Alice showed me in case I ever had to deal with deranged fans."

"That's my girl," Alice says, putting an arm around her.

"I eased over to my bunk and grabbed a can of hairspray and a lighter," Holly continues. "But as I reached both, regular Corey woke up and bit me on the arm."

"Damn," Keren says.

"Totally," Holly agrees. "Then Davey bit me on the leg. I thought I was toast, but I could, like, at least fry them before I died so they wouldn't eat you, too."

"So, what happened?" Lina asks.

"I blazed them all!" Holly says, triumphant. "But when I looked at my wounds, the black lines weren't worming up my veins as fast as with Grover or the others. It was as if the burning aerosol vacuumed it out. I tied tourniquets above each wound and they stopped the spread."

Everyone stares at Holly, amazed.

"Can we use that to save these other people?" Keren asks.

"I mean, maybe?" Holly says. "But we'd need a ton of hairspray. I only had two cans in the bus."

As if to punctuate her remark, the back of the bus explodes, throwing the Roxies off their feet, the fire finally reaching the gas tank.

"And now I don't even have those," Holly says.

"I know where we can find a ton of hairspray," Raquel says. "Like, a ton-a ton."

The bus a burning hulk, Raquel leads the Roxies a short distance through the madness to a backstage storage building off the midway. It's filled with cheap prizes for the carnival games, from stuffed animals to plastic combs—just nothing remotely suitable to fight monsters with. It's there the Roxies learn that Raquel and her late friend, Molly, had summer jobs at the amusement park.

"We ran the rope-ladder climb and ring-toss concessions," Raquel explains. "Get a ring around froggy, and win a stuffed animal? Anyway, the face paint booth was next door. They use hairspray to set the paint and glitter and go through dozens of cans a day. There are so many cases of it, they have the kids sit on them when there's no room for chairs."

"So, what's the plan?" Alice asks, nodding to Holly. "We can't possibly spray all of them. You think it'll work if we start a big hairspray bonfire and decoy them into getting close?"

"Not really?" Holly says. "The burning aerosol will plume out in every direction, but mostly straight up. If we want to get all of them, we have to get them *over* the fire."

No one has any idea how to do this. One by one, they look to Lina. She sighs as if realizing any plan is up to her, then turns to

Raquel. "Do you have any idea how to run the rides around here?"

"No, but they post the instructions next to most of the controls, as they're always having to move operators from one ride to another."

"Good enough," Lina says, turning to Keren. "I have an idea. But we're going to need our instruments, access to the amusement park's PA system, and all the wood we can find."

"Um, okay," Keren says. "What about the undead cannibals?"

Lina nods to the rows of prizes behind them. "Alice? Do you still have your switchblade?"

It takes some doing, but Alice, a veteran of Los Angeles public schools, hollows out five of the super-sized, seldom-to-never awarded stuffed animals. The ground is littered with fluff. The group squeezes themselves into the improvised anti-bite suits, with Alice moving between each to widen or elongate holes to allow for breathing, sight, and movement.

"This is hardly foolproof," Lina acknowledges from inside her improvised dolphin costume. "But if one of those monsters attacks from out of nowhere, they'll bite fluff instead of flesh. Now, Alice? You, Holly, and Raquel hit the midway and get the hairspray. Keren and I will grab a hand truck and get the instruments and amps from the amphitheater. Cool?"

Everyone hesitates. Stepping back into the madness outside the storage building door is no one's favorite plan.

"Come on," Keren finally says. "People need our help."

The group splits up, Alice leading her team to the midway as Keren, tripping over her own feet in a giant pink bear suit, chases after Lina back to the amphitheater. The number of marauding cannibal teens has thinned out. As if they'd had to expand their hunting ground after running out of prey.

*Thank goodness for small mercies*, Keren thinks.

They near the amphitheater, and she glances at the roller coaster line where it all started. The coaster itself looks fine, but the construction site behind it where the park's new garage is being built looks as if part of it has sunk into the ground.

A strange purplish glow emanates from the center of the dig.

Lina grabs Keren's arm, snapping her back into reality. "Hey, pay attention," she says, nodding to the back of the amphitheater. "If we're going to run into any of those undead cannibals, it's going to be here. Stay sharp."

The lights are still up, but they only make the shadows longer and more jagged as the pair creep down the aisles to the stage. The rows of seats are covered in the evidence of the earlier carnage, blood drying around overworked drains. Chunks of flesh and gore piled alongside empty soda cups and abandoned purses and bags. The smell is overwhelming.

By the time they reach the stage, Keren has tears in her eyes.

"There's a hand truck in our dressing room," Lina suggests, unplugging her guitar and setting it next to Alice's bass. "Call out if you get attacked by cannibals."

Grateful to get away from the sight of the massacre, Keren gingerly steps backstage. The tunnel is empty and the backstage area silent. Anyone who was back here is long gone. The dressing room door is only 20 yards away. She figures she can make it there and back in under a minute.

She hurries anyway, the bear suit almost tripping her a few times. She can't believe the Roxies were all back here only a couple of hours ago talking about breaking up. How swiftly things changed—

"Hello, Keren," says a rasp of a voice as she pushes through the dressing room door.

It's a pale, blood-soaked man with tourniquets tied up and down his arms and legs, stomach and chest, and even a last one around his neck. He's been bitten several times and many of his veins throb black, but the bindings keep the darkness from reaching his head.

It's Thad. He snarls at Keren while raising the dressing room phone.

"It's dead," he hisses before dropping it back on its cradle.

*So are you*, Keren thinks.

"You left me behind," Thad says, barely able to breathe through his constricted windpipe.

"We were scared," Keren admits, glancing around for the hand truck. "I'm sorry."

"I mean your solo deal," he says, scoffing. "I could've made you a star. A huge star."

How can he be thinking about that now?

The hand truck is near the door. She edges over to it. "Thad, let me call you an ambul—"

"No," he snaps. "I've heard enough from you. At least I'll die knowing you're my first."

"What...?" Keren asks, confused.

Thad releases all the tourniquets. The black plasma races through the open veins to his brain. Weak before, Thad now leaps to his feet and stares wild-eyed at Keren.

Oh. God.

She grabs the hand truck and hurtles it out into the corridor. The truck is light, but the bear suit is cumbersome. Keren falls against the wall, rights herself, and keeps pushing forward, only to half-trip as she nears the stage.

She's almost to the door when Thad tackles her. He's surprisingly strong for someone half-dead. He holds her against the ground and bites into the bear suit behind her neck. She tries to shake him off, but he's too driven. It's like fighting a grizzly. Ironic. She leans up, only for him to bash her head down onto the concrete. Even with the stuffing buffer of the bear's head, Keren is still dazed.

"Thad...*no*," she murmurs, his teeth getting ever closer to her neck.

The Roxies' manager won't be denied. He continues his assault until Keren can feel his hot breath through the straining polyester fibers at the base of her neck. In what she expects to be the last second of her life, she imagines what this horrific night would be like translated into a song.

One she'll never get to write.

There's a loud bang, followed by running footsteps. Thad grunts. There's a second sound, this one like the crunch of bones and muscle. Thad's weight is suddenly off her prone body.

It's Lina.

"You okay?" Lina asks, lifting Keren's head. A broken guitar is in her hand.

Keren turns to see Thad, nearly decapitated and sprawled in a bloody heap by the wall.

"I am now," Keren says, allowing Lina to help her to her feet.

They load the hand truck with the instruments, amps, and mic, then roll them from the amphitheater to the coaster. Alice, Holly, and Raquel, the latter's penguin suit now covered in blood from beak to feet, are already waiting with cases of hairspray.

"Whoa, what happened to you?" Lina asks Raquel.

"Not my blood," she chirps. "Ready to go for a ride?"

Everyone looks to the top of the roller coaster. The highest point, a narrow service platform right before a high drop, is easily 400 feet above the ground.

"Let's get to it," Lina says.

Lina and Alice load the instruments into the coaster cars, Raquel rewires the sound system while Keren and Holly pile trash below the platform. Only once does a cannibal teen wander over to attack, lunging at Holly though she's able to blast him with her improvised flamethrower.

"Sorry!" she yells to the smoldering corpse. "If you'd waited until later, I could've saved you!"

Alice pats her on her leopard behind. "Can't save 'em all, babe."

"I can try!" Holly replies.

Once the trash pile is built, they empty out the 200-plus cans of hairspray on top of it. Alice stares at it, shaking her head.

"I've seen what happens when one can is thrown on the fire," she says. "This'll be massive."

Everyone climbs into the coaster cars, Raquel switching the ride setting to maintenance before hopping in herself. Keren takes Lina's hand, and the cars begin to slowly ascend the first hill. The view is astounding. They can see well beyond the theme park to the brightly lit Dallas skyline with its distinctive, microphone-shaped Reunion Tower, but also over into Arlington Stadium next door where the Texas Rangers play a night game.

Everywhere but the theme park, from the highway to the stadium, looks monster-free.

They reach the service platform, and Raquel trips the manual brake. The cars jolt to a stop. Alice hops out and is the first to shed her stuffed animal costume. Keren raises an eyebrow. Alice shrugs.

"I can't play in that thing," she says. "And if they can get all the way up here, I want to die looking good *and* sounding great."

Keren snorts and throws off her bear suit as everyone else sheds their costumes, too. They set up their amps and help Holly set up her drum kit as Raquel plugs them into the park's PA system. And as a cool summer breeze blasts around them, they kick off their second possibly-last-concert-ever of the night with the galloping, rapid-fire drumbeat of *Unloved*.

"Are you ready?" Keren yells to an imagined audience. "Then let's *go!*"

They blast through the song, Lina and Alice stepping to Keren's mic for three-part harmony on the chorus, as the Roxies' music booms out wider and farther than it ever has before. The coaster trestles shake under Holly's percussive drumming. When they finish *Unloved*, Keren doesn't even have to so much as raise an eyebrow for the others to start *Suffer the Children*.

After the last note fades, Raquel points. "Here they come."

Hundreds, if not thousands of the cannibalistic undead gather below the roller coaster, flooding in from all sides. Some try to ascend by ladder, others climb right up the trestles, while more attempt to come up the tracks. It'll be only minutes before they reach the band.

"Should we light the fire?" Lina asks.

"Not yet," Holly says. "We have to get all the bees in one place if we want to poison the hive."

They launch into a third song. More and more of the undead converge on the coaster. They climb the vertical loops, the interlocking corkscrew, the dive drop, and the various hills, all aiming for the high platform on which the Roxies perform. One gets within a few yards of the band by pulling itself up the life chain. Holly hurls a drumstick at its head with remarkable precision, sending it sliding back down.

Only when she's out of drumsticks and hitting the snare with the palms of her hand does she nod to Raquel. "Light it up."

Raquel sets their highly flammable animal costumes on fire and kicks them off the side. They drop like blazing comets to the waiting trash pile below, trailing tufts of burning fluff in their wake.

Alice watches then glances to Holly. "How soon unti—"

The explosion that cuts off Alice's words lights up the night as if it was midday. The heat generated rises up to the Roxies, practically singing Keren's eyelashes. The smell of the burning aerosol is overpowering, somewhere between sickeningly sweet and the petrichor of rain. A pink mushroom cloud radiates out from below the coaster, past the parking lot, and onto the highway.

Within seconds, cries of surprise and fear pierce the darkness as the undead, many chewed and grievously injured but alive, regain their consciousness.

"Everybody remain calm!" Lina yells into Keren's microphone. "People below, please help those still trapped on the Cyclone to get to the ground."

This does little to calm the crowd. But people do hurry over and assist those on the coaster back to solid ground. Soon, everyone descends in an orderly fashion to safety.

"You guys did it!" Raquel says.

"*We* did it," Keren counters. "If this doesn't make you an honorary Roxie, I don't know will."

Alice scoffs. "All this because you planned to go solo."

"Yeah, I think it's clear I wouldn't last two seconds out in the big world without you girls," Keren replies. "I'm going to call Bel-Air and wriggle out of the contract."

"Nah, don't do that," Alice says. "When you fall on your ass, it'll make you appreciate us that much more. You hear Mick Jagger's solo record earlier this year? *Woof.* Bet he loves Keith now."

Keren turns to Lina even as the guitarist steps over to hug her.

"You okay?" Lina asks.

"Yeah, you?"

"I am now—"

The coaster rattles and shakes. A sound like thunder rumbles up from the ground. The people below scream in panic.

"What's happening?" Alice asks. "Did the fire weaken the trestles?"

Keren's gaze turns to the nearby construction site. The faint purple glow she glimpsed earlier isn't so faint now. It grows larger as it nears the surface. Large cracks in the ground widen as gray-black smoke plumes out. The people nearest breathe it in. Almost instantly, they revert to their wild-eyed, black-veined undead version, hungry again for human flesh.

"Oh, God," Keren whispers as great tentacles slither from the earthen maw.

"We have to get off this thing, fast!" Lina yells, waving everyone back into the coaster cars.

Raquel releases the brakes, and the cars fly over the precipice before zipping down the coaster's first peak. Three squid-like tentacles lined with oozing suckers whip out of the crevice below and swing past their heads, the Roxies ducking low to avoid being struck.

Keren, exhilarated and bewildered, holds Lina's hand and closes her eyes as they fly through this night without end.

## Hip To Be Scared
Darren Gordon Smith
& Staci Layne Wilson

1. [dgs]

"I love this, it's so *real,*" she said, surveying the graffiti, the jagged bottles littering what was left of the sidewalks, and shirtless men riding circles on kids' bikes.

"Uh-huh."

He said it in a way that made her wonder whether he didn't believe her, or if he was quoting from one of his favorite John Hughes movies. She tugged a strand of her blue hair that a strong, balmy wind had blown out of place. "I mean it, like *totally.*"

They laughed. Maddie and Monroe had only known each other for a few days, but they were like *so* in sync. They both hung around "Raddies"—kids who were enthralled by the Awesome Eighties—but neither of them had ever dated anyone else with the same level of passion for the best-era-ever before.

"My street is only a few blocks over, and it's not as sketchy," Monroe said.

"But I *love* sketchy!" Maddie stopped to catch her breath. The hill from the bus stop was steeper than she'd anticipated, and her eBay-bought Jellies pinched her toes. This paradise looked just like *To Live and Die in L.A.* to her.

Monroe was also huffing, but still managed to give her his best Max Headroom grin. Though beads of sweat rolled down his forehead, his Flock of Seagulls sprouting hair still looked perfect. He led her on his shortcut, a severe dogleg through a series of alleyways.

"Whoa, look!" She stopped and pointed to a middle-aged man two houses down. He had spiky Sting-length hair, only his was dyed black. And oily, like Ronald Reagan's. He was rolling a trash can to the curb. "It couldn't be him, right?

"Who, Adam Ant?"

"No, silly. Rory Weedham!"

Monroe took another look, just a quick glance. In this neighborhood, you don't get too nosy. "I thought he was dead or something."

Actually, nobody knew for sure what really happened to him. Weedham, a techno/glam/postpunk artist who came on the UK music scene in the late 1970s, had a series of underground hits until announcing his retirement in 1983. At first, no one believed he really was going to quit the music biz, least of all his record company. Surely that was some publicity gimmick. But when he came back from his North American tour and announced to the press that he was done with music and Maggie Thatcher's England, and that he was "going to disappear," he'd meant it. Literally.

In the intervening years, even Rory's close friends said that they'd had contact with him on only a handful of occasions. And none of them had heard from him since 1993—except his brother Rhys, the famed music producer for Russell Aquarius, who said that Rory left a message on his voice mail on September 10, 2001, warning Rhys to leave New York City "before it was too late." (Sadly, Rhys ignored his younger brother's warning, and his teenage wife was killed when one of the Twin Towers fell and destroyed their loft in Tribeca.)

Before Monroe could warn Maddie that she shouldn't talk to strangers in his neighborhood, especially at night, she ran across the street and over to the guy's house. The young man tried to run after her, but the light at the corner went green and the SWOOSH! of traffic blocked his way.

The bristly-haired late middle-ager eyed Maddie with suspicion. He dug this young bird's trendy getup, but if this was another bullshit paternity scam, he had no time for that.

"Excuse me, but are you –"

"No," he curtly interrupted before she could even finish her question.

"Oh, I'm sorry, I thought you might be Rory Weedham. He was... or is—"

"I know who he was."

"Well, anyway, you look younger than he would be if, you know, he's really still alive." She looked confused. "Strange, though, just like Rory, your accent... it's Yorkshire, right?"

Rory started to dig this girl now. She seemed sincere—and cute as a bloody button, even if her hair looked like it could use a lot more gel. Why not tell her the truth? He came closer and whispered, "Okay, you got me: Rory in the flesh."

He was about to ask her to come in when Monroe dashed in from across the street.

"Hey 'Roe," she said, looking up. "It *is* him."

"Shhhh," said Rory. "Who's this guy, your boyfriend?"

The two looked at each other in embarrassed silence. How could they define their profound yet only less than weeklong relationship? "Ummm..." they said in unison.

"Mate, that almost had me fooled," said Rory, pointing to the device in Monroe's hand. It was an iPhone with a case made to look like a Sony Walkman, and a faux tape inside titled, in a handwriting style font, "Tubular Mix Tape, a registered trademark."

Monroe frowned. "I *wish* it was the real thing. Damn! I wish I'd been living back when people used those things."

"Me, too," said Maddie, "Back in the '80s people were like, living in the moment, and getting all outrageous. Not like all this self-conscious crap going on now.'"

Rory smiled. Either a rare dentist in England had taken care of the man's pearly white teeth, or he'd gotten a nice new set in Beverly Hills. "There was plenty of yam-up-your-ass self-consciousness in those days too, and let me tell you, most of it was rot. Plus, back then, everyone was sitting around bored, arguing about who was in what movie. Basically, we were all just waiting for the internet to be invented."

"But the fashion was so cool!" argued Monroe.

"And the music was awesome!" added Maddie.

Rory, of course, agreed about some of the music, but couldn't seem to convince the young couple that everything in the 1980s was not better. What they saw as a more innocent time was to him just a cynical backlash against the more progressive 1960s and '70s. If he had a schilling for every 20-something here in L.A. who thought life in the '80s was better, well—he'd be richer than he was now. Not that money and fame meant fuck-all to him anyway.

The one-time pop star wrung his hands in frustration. But just as Maddie feared that she and her new beau had pissed him off, he gave them a weird smile and invited them in.

Once inside, the young couple looked around Rory's house in awe as he ushered them through the hallways. From the outside, the place looked like just another modest Hollywood bungalow. Inside, though, it was massive. The furnishings in the foyer and hallways were ornate, and the place was covered with antiques of just about every era: a Louis XIV settee, medieval armor, a Palm Pilot from the 1990s.

Rory led them deeper, downstairs, and into the den. The room looked like Steve Jobs' wet dream: painted from floor to ceiling in a no-bullshit white, including the only two items in it, an Eames chair and a plastic love seat. Rory offered them the love seat. He took the chair.

"Anyone want a beer?" Rory asked.

Maddie and Monroe were just out of college and always looking for a rad time, especially on the cheap—so yeah, of course they did.

He reached down to a hidden spot behind the chair, grabbed a couple bottles of Newcastle, and passed them out. Rory popped one open for himself too.

The couple told Rory their names, and many toasts were made as the three of them knocked off an entire case of ale.

Monroe belched, followed by a big long one from Maddie. She spilled beer on her shirt, then used her skirt to wipe her mouth. She didn't bother fixing her skirt after that, and Monroe didn't even notice.

Rory did, but said nothing. Of course, he wasn't drunk. What kind of Englishman would get pissed from a dozen pints? All the while, Rory got weirder and weirder. He talked of UFOs, aliens and elves, before turning to his favorite subject: time travel.

While Monroe held on to Maddie in a vain effort to stop the room from spinning, Rory claimed that he'd seen the future in 1983—Reagan getting re-elected, the explosion of The Challenger, the stock market crash, and the future ubiquity of actress Daryl Hannah, and decided to quit the '80s before, he said, it was too late. He admitted to going back to that time period occasionally for shits and giggles and Peruvian cocaine.

Rory reached under his chair again, this time coming out with an ivory-colored keytar—a mobile synthesizer that could be worn like an electric guitar. He held it close up so they could see that it was hand-signed by Gary Numan and Kate Bush.

His guests gasped in amazement.

"I bet you this baby," Rory said, pointing to his precious synth, "and my Keds worn by both members of Wang Chung, that the two of you couldn't stand to live through even *one* weekend in the '80s."

Monroe downed his eighth pint. "Fuck that," he slurred, "Those '80s guys couldn't handle a goddam two days here in our shithole we call the 21st century."

"Amen!" Maddie cried and gave a wink, two things she knew she did when she was shitfaced. But she was tired of beer. She asked Rory what else he had to drink.

Rory produced a bottle of Jim Beam whiskey from seemingly out of nowhere. They all downed shots. "So," he asked them, "are you guys up for the bet?"

"Why the hell not?" Maddie asked, lifting her shirt to wipe her mouth again. "You can't lose betting on an impossibility." She knew that made little sense, but c'mon, who's ever gonna prove that she couldn't hack the '80s?

Monroe belched again, this time dribbling out some ale. "Fuck yeah! Whatever she said!"

"Well, okay, then," said Rory, "Let's get started." He pulled out his iPhone. "Let's see, today is August 19th. Okay, according to my calendar, I played The Troubadour on August 21, 1983. You guys meet me at the Troub at 9 p.m. in two days, and you win your bet."

"What do we win in this ridiculous bet?" asked Maddie.

"Like I said, if you last a whole weekend in 1983, you get the keytar and the sneakers."

"Hold on," said Monroe, in a brief flash of sobriety. "If we *lose* this crazy bet, what happens then?"

"Then," said Rory with a sly smile, "I get your girlfriend."

"She's not my g—"

"Shut up, 'Roe," said Maddie, elbowing him in the ribs. "He *is* my boyfriend, and we're very much in love, right, honey?"

Monroe looked confused.

"Nice one, Maddie," grinned Rory. "Who are you trying to convince?"

"Well, you, obviously," she said. "First of all, I'm not a piece of meat to be bartered in a bet, and secondly, c'mon, how old are you?"

"I'm a very fit 66 years old," said Rory, slapping his stomach as if for proof.

"Still, you're more than twice my age, and that's just gross."

"Think of it this way," said Rory. "I'm not really that age because of all the time travel I've done over the last few decades. And in the '80s, I'm at least 40 years younger."

Maddie had no patience for any kind of self-serving pretzel logic. She'd heard all that crap before from her history professor, who was always making passes at her. "What the hell does that even mean, Rory?!"

"Fuckin'-A, man," Monroe interjected. "This is like *Back to the Future*, parts 1 through 10!"

Rory shook his head. "Please don't insult me. Time travel with a DeLorean has always been problematic. I mean, if it really worked, John DeLorean would've hightailed it after he was busted at the Bonaventure with a suitcase of blow and out on bail. Me? I spent years perfecting my method—and I studied physics under Dr. Brian May."

"Yeah, and I learned orthodontics with Freddie Mercury," snapped Maddie. "Anyway, if there actually *was* a time machine, I'd go back to the '80s and stay there forever."

"And she still wouldn't fuck you!" added Monroe.

"Amen!" said Maddie, with a wink at no one in particular.

"Then the bet's on," said Rory. He stood up and stuffed wads of cash into their pockets. "I'm giving each of you a thousand bucks—which, back in 1983, was good money. He reached under his chair and pulled out a set of harnesses and two old-fashioned aviator's goggles. "Now, put these on."

"You're one crazy old dude," said Maddie, smiling as she and Monroe strapped up their gear. They were game for any mindfuck the old Brit cooked up. And they were drunk.

"Just remember, if you can't hack the '80s, then you meet me in New York tomorrow— well, Saturday, 1983, at the Chelsea Hotel instead. You've got more than enough dough to catch a flight." Rory turned dead serious. "More likely though, if you don't keep your wits about you, the '80s will kill you."

Maddie laughed. The idea that a decade could kill anyone, let alone her, cracked her up.

Monroe laughed too, though he wasn't really sure why.

Rory moved his chair, revealing a firefighter's pole and a passageway beneath it. He slid down the pole, with Maddie and Monroe following him.

They descended into the darkness. Maddie and Monroe felt their bodies pitch until they were flipped upside down and curled into fetal positions.

Finally, with a PLUNK!, they fell onto a floor. The place looked like Rory's den, only the walls were covered with wood paneling, the chair was an open-oval wicker basket suspended from the ceiling, and there was a sheepskin cover on the love seat.

2. [slw]

"Where's the old dude?" Maddie asked, looking around the den, wide-eyed. The goggles she'd been wearing had disappeared.

Monroe felt inside his front pockets. The cash rustled. Could this actually be real? He pulled the bills out and looked at them, carefully noting the year on each one. Not one was dated past 1983.

Maddie stood woozily. "I don't feel so good," she announced. "How much did we drink?"

"Either too much, or not enough," Monroe said. He got to his feet. He slipped his hand inside his left back pocket. Empty. So was the right. "Damn! I lost my phone."

Maddie checked for hers. "Me, too."

"Come on, let's get out of here before that man comes back. I don't think he was Rory Weedham. Probably some deranged old fuck who drugged us."

Maddie shuddered. "I'm not so sure."

"Why?"

Maddie didn't reply. Instead, she turned and padded across the shag carpet. Monroe followed, and they made their way quickly out of the house.

They shut the door behind them, finding themselves alone in the dark. The neighborhood was quiet—it must have been sometime in the middle of the night.

"Like I said, I live just a few blocks over." Monroe took Maddie's hand and led her down the deserted sidewalk.

They'd gone about half a block when Maddie stopped and gestured to the hulks of parked cars. "Notice anything?" Monroe peered at them, cocking his head. He shrugged. "They're old. All of them." She looked up at the streetlamps and telephone poles. "See any cell towers?"

Monroe felt a chill in his suddenly pounding heart. "Holy shit." He took a deep breath. "But wait. This could still be bull. Or maybe we're tripping balls."

"Maybe," Maddie said, unconvinced.

Monroe tugged at her hand, and they continued down the street toward his house. Another check of his back pockets confirmed they were empty, which meant he'd lost his house keys too. But one of his seven roommates would let them in.

When they got to the house, Monroe stopped and stared. It looked different, somehow. The outside was paneled, not stucco, and there was only one car in the driveway—a 1980s model Ford Escort that looked brand new. Monroe and his friends all drove Priuses or rode bicycles. He peered at the house number, wondering if he'd somehow gone to the wrong place. But no. The address was correct, and the shape of the structure was the same. He took a deep breath and walked up the trio of steps to the front porch. He knocked. Maddie waited on the lawn, eying him with uncertainty.

When there was no immediate answer, Monroe knocked again. He yelled out softly, "It's me, Monroe. I lost my keys."

The front door flew open, and Monroe found himself face-to-face with a 40-something wearing a mullet and a scowl. The man held a gun.

"Oh, shit!" Monroe turned and dashed off the porch and onto the lawn. He grabbed Maddie's hand, and together they broke into a run.

They ran until they hit Sunset Boulevard. No matter what the year, the landmark Strip was unmistakable. There were The Roxy and The Rainbow, right next door to each other. And another place, Gazzarri's, could be seen a few blocks down to their right. They were all closed, and only a few cars could be seen cruising the boulevard.

"Is that... Gazzarri's?" Maddie gasped. "It can't be."

"They shut down in the early '90s," Monroe said, panting. "I read about it on the Raddies Facebook group a few weeks ago. It was a hot place in the '80s, though. All the cool bands played there—WASP, Twisted Sister, KIX, Ratt... you name it."

"You like hair-metal?" Maddie said, scrunching her face. "But *your* hair..."

"Flock of Seagulls, I know." Monroe said. "But I do have a stash of spandex pants and half-shirts that I wear on... special occasions." He gave her his best come-hither look.

"Ew! Gag me with a spoon," Maddie said. Then she grinned. "Can you believe it? We're actually here. 1983! It's so gnarly!" Then she yawned. "I'm tired." She felt in her pockets and found the wad of cash Rory had given her. "Let's walk to the nearest hotel and check in." She paused. "I hope they won't need I.D."

"In the 1980s? Not a chance. Things were so much looser, so much cooler then—er, now."

As they walked, Maddie noticed the trash thrown in the gutters and the band flyers stapled to all the telephone poles—the papers were three and four sheets deep, if not more, and they stretched from the ground to beyond eye-level. And there was a smell. Like exhaust and hairspray, but also an indefinable stench.

The air even felt thick. "Is that *smog*?"

"I don't know," Monroe said. As they passed the Whisky a Go-Go, he pointed up at the street sign. "Mötley Crüe lived on Clark Street in the early '80s. I wish I could remember the exact address."

They walked on and soon found themselves standing in front of a rather seedy-looking motel. It was painted pink and looked like it had seen better days. But they thought it wise to stay under the radar until they could figure things out. They wouldn't be carded here, and their cash would be more than acceptable.

It was, and as hoped, the clerk didn't look at them twice, let alone ask for I.D.

As soon as they entered their room—using an actual key!—Maddie flopped herself onto the bedspread. "Oh, God, I could sleep for a decade." She stretched, and then wrinkled her nose. "Why didn't you ask for a non-smoking room?"

Monroe shrugged. "No such thing in the early '80s."

She breathed in even more deeply. "Ahhh. The '80s aroma." Then she sat up. "Let's turn on the TV. I want to see *The A-Team*, *Mama's Family*, and *Trapper John, MD*... all airing now, for the first time!"

Once they got the ancient tube TV to work, the only show they could find was a rebroadcast of the evening news. All the other stations were off for the night.

They cuddled under the cigarette-burned covers, watching in amazement as a red-faced, white-haired anchor named Jerry Dunphy recited stories about racial tensions, cop killings, homelessness, the AIDS epidemic, Ira Gershwin's death, and the torching of a local synagogue. There were no reports on anything rad at all.

3. [dgs]

Monroe was tired, or so he said, and asked Maddie to turn off the TV so he could get some sleep. He was so agitated by whatever drug that crazy Brit must've given them that he just wanted to close his eyes.

Maddie turned off the TV just as the guy was blabbering about there being no end in sight for the economic recession and the hit to the local job market. Though the news was totally depressing, she wanted to watch until the station signoff—another thing from the era she had to experience. She turned off the tube and looked around for a radio. There was one built into the wall, along with an intercom, but it didn't work.

Oh well, there were a million other things to do in 1983! Sure, it was one thing to get in a Patty Smyth costume and go to AwesomeCon, where she'd get fly on the dance floor to Grandmaster Flash along with her Raddie friends, who'd come dressed as their favorite *A.L.F.* character. But here and now, she could experience the real deal!

She peered through the bars on the window to watch the motel's intermittently flashing PAY TV! sign. The realness of it all made her aware of certain needs. If a decade could be said to be an object of sexual fantasy, the '80s was it for Maddie. She climbed into bed and nuzzled up to the current object of her affection.

Monroe was too scared to think about sex. Yet, he was too scared to tell Maddie no. Once Maddie had mounted him, his thoughts began to wander. Didn't Uncle Gregg once tell him that back in the '80s, it was considered "bogus" to turn down free coke or free sex with a babe, whether you were in the mood to do it or not? Or maybe Uncle Gregg didn't say it, but it was said about him at his funeral? Then he wondered why he was thinking about that dickhead right now instead of his own.

Maddie didn't notice her lover's distractedness and it wasn't out of sexual pleasure. She, too, was distracted. Shouldn't he be wearing a condom, with herpes, and who knows what, back in the day? *But Monroe's not really from the '80s*, she thought, and he'd been here with her this whole time, so where would he have gotten herpes?

After a few more strokes, Maddie came to realize that intercourse wasn't going to work out for her tonight. She stopped and told Monroe that she was going out to find an ice machine.

"Okay," he said. He wondered what she needed ice for, but he was happy to be left in peace, at least for a bit.

His head was spun, replaying—forward and backwards—the night with Rory, or whoever he was. Then his mind turned to Maddie. The past few days with her had been intoxicating, but he wasn't about to get his heart broken like with Martha, a petite young woman that he met when she was playing Carla in a *Cheers* shadow cast. And he was just starting to enjoy being single again. At all the Totally '80s parties he'd go to around town, more than a few smoking-hot women had asked him out. Anyway, Maddie wasn't really his type. She was pretty, for sure, but blondes with blue highlights weren't his thing. He'd masturbated to his young Demi Moore poster enough times to know what his type was.

Maddie closed the door and looked around for something rad. There was a parking lot but there were only clunkers, the kind that would've been totally old even back then. She spied a dark alleyway; on the other side was Sunset, of course, but whereas the alley looked sketchy, the Boulevard was suicide.

She decided to head for the light. That was the sole illumination around, a desk lamp in the innkeeper's bulletproof office that passed for the "lobby." Luckily for her, the surly pockmarked man who checked them in was no longer there. Instead, there was a dark-haired girl about Maddie's age.

When she saw Maddie looking at her, she smiled. The girl opened the scratched-up Plexiglas-covered porthole to talk to her. "I love your hair!" she told Maddie. "Manic Panic?"

They compared bracelets, and soon they were bonding over earrings and shoes. The clerk said her name was Jaia. She'd graduated early from Hollywood High thanks to top grades, and planned to make her dad proud by attending MIT in the fall. All she knew was she *loved* music and two guys: Ian Curtis, and Rory Weedham. Sadly, Ian was dead by his own hand. But Rory was alive and one day, sooner or later, she *knew* she was going to meet him. Jaia said she loved super-dark music and to her, he was it: more techno than Gary Numan, darker than Einstürzende Neubauten, and less hopeful than Joy Division.

It turned out that they shared a lot of the same musical tastes, though Maddie figured she shouldn't say anything about having met Rory for fear that would somehow ruin everything and she'd not be allowed in the '80s anymore.

Maddie asked the girl whether she knew of any after-hours clubs around here that she could party at. Jaia clapped her hands in excitement. "I'm just about to close up. Hang here for five, and I'll take you to the gnarliest fucking private club you've ever seen."

She opened the back door in the office to reveal the living quarters she shared with her family. While she was back there, presumably changing clothes and freshening up, Maddie could see through the open door the silhouette of the surly, pockmarked man watching what appeared to be a third-generation bootleg video of *T.J. Hooker*. She could hear snoring. The old man must've fallen asleep while watching one of William Shatner's most sensitive and nuanced performances as the Lake City cop.

An extended TV car chase later, Jaia came outside looking like a babe to the max. Within a few minutes, she had teased and sprayed her long and curly brunette locks and donned a short, sexy red dress with shoulder pads that, even for Maddie, were way too big. She thought the dress made Jaia look like a cross between Jennifers Beal, Grey, and Connelly—with a touch of Joe Montana. On second glance, she realized her new friend looked a little like Demi Moore. And she had the certain, sexy, slo-mo poise of a Phoebe Cates splashing in a pool. Monroe had confessed to her the other day about his Demi Moore fixation, so Maddie made a mental note not to introduce Jaia to him.

Jaia added another bracelet, and announced she was ready to go. "C'mon!"

Maddie followed Jaia to a rust-covered and beat-up VW Thing with no windshield or windows. They got in the car, and with a SWOOSH of Santa Ana wind to their faces, they were off.

4.  [slw]

"Whoa, what is this place?" Maddie asked, wide-eyed.

They were in the basement of an old hotel in Downtown Los Angeles's skid row. The girls had entered through a service door in the piss-soaked back alley after giving the gatekeeper the secret password: Grody.

Jaia smiled. "This is the darkest of dark places. Not only is it a cesspool of hookers, pushers, bums, addicts, thieves, murderers, and DMV employees, it is also haunted. Yep, that's right. The Black Dahlia had her last cocktail here before being murdered in Hollywood in the '40s, and they say she still hangs around here."

"Rad," Maddie said. She glanced around while trying not to breathe in too much black mold and asbestos, then asked, "Where's the party?"

"Follow me."

Maddie followed Jaia's big, bright dress down a long, spooky corridor, through an abandoned employee locker room, and to a large double door. Jaia cocked her head, listening. She motioned for Maddie to come closer. She focused. She could hear music, but it sounded like it was coming from well beyond the door and a long way down. She looked quizzically at her new friend.

"That's the party." Jaia reached up into her huge, stiff mane and extracted a hairpin. She jammed it into the lock and wiggled it around. "This is the fun part."

Maddie covertly rolled her eyes. If this was the fun part, what must the party within be like?

The lock gave, and Jaia opened the door.

The room was dark, but Maddie did see a square of light in the floor. "Is that a trap door?"

She grinned and nodded, her braces gleaming despite the gloom. "Yes, the parties are always in the subbasement. We're going to have to stoop down the whole time we're in there, but it's hella tubular. And there's supposed to be a new band playing tonight."

Maddie shrugged and walked to the door in the floor. Jaia bent down and moved a section of crunchy carpet aside, found the recessed handle, then gave it an upward pull. The sound of a live band burst forth, as did the clinks of glasses, lots of buzzing, and shrill laughter.

The girls clambered down the ladder and found themselves thrown into the chaos of a violent slam-dance. Groomed for doom, the punkers wore steel-toed Doc Martens, safety-pinned holey jeans, distressed band tees, spiked bracelets and chokers. Even their Mohawks were domed into sharp, sprayed ax-blade points.

While being pummeled, stepped on, and spat on, the two made their way to the bar. They collapsed onto the low barstools, caught their breaths, then ordered drinks—a Blue Lagoon for Maddie and a Screaming Orgasm for Jaia.

"Cheers!" they chirped in unison while touching glasses.

Then another glass joined the toast. "Hey, ladies," said the 40-something buttinsky. He was short enough to stand without stooping in the cavernous subbasement, wore a suit with loafers, designer shades, and had an egregious combover lacquered with so much hairspray you could bounce a quarter off it.

"Oh, hey," Maddie said with as little enthusiasm as she could muster.

Jaia's reaction was just the opposite. "Oh, Philly! I'm so glad you're here, dude. This is my new friend. Isn't she awesome? Maddie, this is Phil... as in Spector. The famous music dude."

Phil basked in the glow of her fandom, kissed her on the cheek, and then extended his soft, plump right hand to Maddie.

She just looked at it. This guy was a gun-toting killer. How was he out in public? Then she remembered he wouldn't commit his most notorious crime for another couple of decades. "Uh, nice to meet you," she said.

Maddie turned her attention to the band. They were awful, but at least it was authentic 1980s music! No auto-tune. No laptops. Just three guys with a drum kit, bass, and mic. They stood on a stage so small it could pass for the head of a pin, but it didn't stop them from bashing away at their instruments like gorillas in an old Samsonite luggage commercial. Maddie had all the Blu-rays, which were in VHS tape-shaped boxed sets, of *Raddest TV Commercials of the Awesome 80s*, and that was one of her favorites. It was a toss-up between that and Wendy's *Where's the Beef?* The singer was snarling into the mic, something about Satan and the price of Nikes. He had long, dark curly hair, and piercing, almost black, brown eyes.

Maddie interrupted the discussion about Phil's gun collection. "Hey, who's the band? That lead singer is hot."

Phil gave a shit-eating grin. "That's my newest discovery. Richard and the Ramirez's. They've got a killer sound, don't they?"

Maddie, who liked nothing better than to Netflix-and-chill with days-long true crime documentary binges, gulped. "Oh, my God. Are we in The Cecil Hotel?"

"Yes, ma'am," Philly confirmed. "It's a historical landmark."

Maddie instantly remembered where she'd heard of The Cecil before. She'd watched *American Horror Story: Hotel* twice, not to mention the many documentaries on the disappearance and mysterious death of Elisa Lam.

"Whoa, this is surreal." She ordered another Blue Lagoon. She savored the frosty mix of Curacao, lemonade, and cheap vodka as she watched Richard perform. The band sucked, but he wasn't half-bad. She tapped Phil on the shoulder, then pointed to the stage. "Can you introduce me after the show?"

"Better than that," the megalomaniacal music producer shouted over the din. "There's an after-party in my room upstairs. Richard's coming, and so are some other friends I'd like you to meet."

Maddie thought of Monroe, back at the motel. He was probably wondering where she was right now. Even in the '80s, ice was ready-made. Her errand wouldn't have taken this long. She pulled Jaia close and said into her ear, "My boyfriend is still at the motel. Is there any way you could get your dad to give him a message? Maybe Monroe can get an Uber and come over here."

"An Uber?"

"A cab. I mean a cab," Maddie clarified.

"That would be hella expensive. My brother Jackson has a motorcycle, and he'd probably give your guy a ride over." Jaia reached into her fanny pack and rummaged around. "I've got change. I'll give Jacks a call." With that, she disappeared into the sea of pogoing punks, leaving Maddie alone with Philly.

While the man went on and on about what an off-the-hook party he'd be throwing later, Maddie's mind wandered to the possibilities. What if she killed Phil Spector and Richard Ramirez? Just think of all the lives she'd save! And while she was at it, she could assassinate Tipper Gore and invest in Microsoft. But she was no killer, and she hadn't a clue how to play the stock market—if it was anything like the movie *Wall Street*, which wasn't even out yet, she wanted no part of it.

Phil was now trying to regale her with the "funny" story of how he pulled a pistol on "that hippie pussy" John Lennon. Maddie thought the least she could do was look up the future victims of misters Spector and Ramirez and warn them. What were their names again? If only she hadn't been forced to leave her iPhone back in the 2020s! But there had to a Yellow Pages somewhere in the hotel. She'd let her "fingers do the walking," as another of her favorite TV commercials said.

Jaia returned with her bright neon pink lipstick smeared, her 'do disheveled, and a loogie hanging from one of her shoulder pads. But she was smiling. "Jacks is bringing Monroe over," she announced.

"Gnarly." So much for her plan to keep 'Roe away from the beauteous brunette, but there was no other way.

Jaia ordered another drink—Sex on the Beach this time—then produced a travel-sized hairspray canister from her fanny-pack so she could re-sculpt her nest of curls.

Maddie watched in horror as Jaia unleashed a gush of environmentally unfriendly aerosol into the air. She held her tongue, but it wasn't easy. She could lecture her new friend on the perils of propellants later. When Jaia fixed her lipstick, Maddie asked if she could borrow it. And some rouge. She felt woefully under made-up with her bare face and flat hair. She wished she had some blue eyeshadow.

The band finished playing, and the punkers rushed the bar. "Let's get out of here," Philly suggested, taking the girls by the hands. He pulled them to the ladder, then helped them up by boosting their butts with the flat of his hand. Jaia didn't bat a lash, but Maddie was seriously considering filing a sexual harassment lawsuit.

Phil huffed his way up, followed by a sweaty, reeking Richard, who was weighed down with a large backpack, and the band.

Three punk girls joined them, and the last one out shut the trapdoor.

The small group took four flights of filthy stairs up to the party room. It was hardly suite-sized, and it was already packed with people. The only place to sit was on the bed, the desk, or the toilet, but those were all claimed. Maddie crab-stepped to the desk and looked in the drawer for a copy of the Yellow Pages.

There was nothing inside other than a Church of Scientology pamphlet and half a pack of Freshen-Up gum. Maddie hummed the jingle, "Here it comes, the gum that goes squirt," and helped herself to a piece. When she bit into it, a small spurt of sugary syrup ejaculated from the rubbery square pouch. She palmed the rest of the pack so Monroe could try it, too.

While she waited for her boyfriend to arrive, Maddie took stock of the partygoers. People of the '80s who weren't on TV were not nearly as impressive as she hoped. They were smaller than she thought they'd be (or maybe they were just engulfed in their oversized clothing and colossal hair). When they laughed, she could see their silver fillings. The olfactive clash of comingling Drakkar Noir and Love's Baby Soft made her feel sick to her stomach. At least the speakers on the boom box were better than an iPhone.

Maddie felt someone's palm against the small of her back. People sure were handsy in the '80s, she thought with annoyance as she faced the person. It was Richard. He grinned at her, exposing rotten teeth.

"Hey, I heard you wanted to meet me?" he said, giving Maddie a leer.

"Ummm—" she stammered. Then *another* guy touched her! Maddie practically gave herself whiplash as she turned to see who else would be named in her sexual harassment lawsuit. It was Monroe. "Oh," she sighed with relief. "It's you. I'm so glad you're here."

Monroe was about to say something, but Richard cut him off. "Who's this?" demanded the pockmarked soon-to-be serial killer, crossing his scrawny arms.

5. [dgs]

Monroe was elated to see Maddie. He'd been worried sick ever since he discovered that she'd left their motel room. Less than an hour ago, he'd been awoken by the insistent knocking of some guy in leather pants, sitting on a motorcycle, who sternly told him, "Come with me, you need to find your girl."

"What? My girl? Where? Is she—"

"We don't have time for small talk. Come out and hop on."

Monroe's Seagulls hair was limp, but since he'd slept in his clothes, he was otherwise ready to go. He jumped on the back of the guy's Honda.

The guy turned to his side. "The name's Jacks, and I got the facts." He kicked on his engine, emitting a rumble like a space liftoff that drowned out all sound. Jacks floored it, and they sped off in a wheelie that kicked over a garbage can near the lobby on the way out.

Monroe clung tightly to Jacks. "Shouldn't we turn around and put the trashcan back?"

"Fuck that!" shouted Jacks, looking askance at Monroe while weaving through traffic. "My old man owns this dump. And fuck him, too."

"Where's Maddie?"

"She died a while ago."

"What?! *My* Maddie?!"

"Who? No, I was talking about my ex," Jacks said with genuine emotion. "She was swallowed by lava. Fucking Mount St. Helens, man.

"I'm sorry to hear that, but where's my girl?"

The motorbike backfired. "I guess she's with my sister at one of those clubs that have no name," said Jacks. "My sister said it was important to pick you up and drop you there."

"Is Maddie hurt or in trouble or something?"

Jacks just shrugged and started zig-zagging the bike along Sunset Boulevard as if it were a slalom course.

For a guy who calls himself Jacks the Facts, thought Monroe, he didn't seem to know much at all. "So, what's the deal about this club with no name?"

"Beats me. I'm sure they play the same shitty music my sister listens to. Me, I'm Michael all the way." He lifted his left hand to show Monroe his fingerless white glove. Jacks grabbed his crotch and did his best *Billie Jean*, further destabilizing the bike.

Before Jacks could go into any more material from *Thriller*, Monroe asked, "Do you always ride without a helmet?"

"You know it, man. I mean, do I wanna look like I 'tard out on the short bus?"

"Huh?"

"Like I don't want to look like a retard."

"Do people still use the R-word here?"

"The R-word? Yeah, man, I mean retard, dimwit, dumbfuck. Where the hell are you from, anyway?"

"You don't want to know."

"Whatever," said Jacks, turning into an alley. He stopped the bike so short that Monroe almost tumbled over the handlebars.

Just then, Jaia emerged from the shadows to meet them.

Jacks bid them both adieu, and with another engine backfire, he was off.

Monroe barely noticed Jacks leave, for he was looking at one of the prettiest girls he'd ever seen. He stammered to her, "Is Maddie okay? Where is she?"

She wiped her nose and giggled. "Follow me." She took his hand and led him through the dark labyrinth.

Monroe liked this girl. She reminded him of someone, but he couldn't place who. He felt a little guilty about enjoying holding the hand of this beautiful young woman when he should be concentrating on making sure Mads was safe. Still, her hand was so soft, and he loved the way she smelled. "What is that scent you're wearing?"

"Anais, Anais."

"I heard you the first time."

They continued their labyrinthine journey, zigging here, zagging there, stooping and occasionally banging their heads on plumbing pipes. They talked about bands they liked, the rap music of Grandmaster Flash, and Dustin Hoffman's performance in *Tootsie.* As her brother had, she asked him where they were visiting from. He wanted to tell her that he too was from L.A., only from another century, but instead replied, "Cleveland."

Eventually, they arrived at the party scene on the fourth floor.

Jaia said hello to a swarthy, well-dressed man walking around with rolled-up currency.

She pointed to her nose and asked Monroe whether he'd like to join them.

He shook his head. "I'm good."

"What the fuck does that mean?" asked the swarthy man.

Jaia shrugged, then the two of them left.

Monroe's eyes had barely adjusted to the light when, though a thick cloud of cigarette smoke and vaporized sweat, he spotted Maddie with some rotten-toothed punk dweeb trying to hit on her.

"Leave the lady alone," Monroe told the guy.

"Heh," Richard laughed with sarcasm, "now she's a *lady*." He turned to Maddie. "Nice meeting you and your gorgeous breasts. See you soon." He took off, flashing Monroe a what-the-fuck-you-gonna-do-about-it smile.

Maddie kissed Monroe. "You're just in the nick of time. Do you know who that was? It's—"

"I was so, so worried about you," Monroe interrupted.

"You were? That's so sweet." She kissed him again. Her breath smelled of vodka and Chardonnay. She filled him in on everything she'd seen so far at this grungy hotel.

A guy behind them asked Monroe to hand him the beer bottle on the windowsill. Monroe gave the guy his drink, and the man thanked him.

"No problem," said Monroe.

The guy looked at him with fury. "'No problem'? Well, I fucking hope so," he said, then took off with his beer and his attitude.

Suddenly, Jaia came back, glass in hand, and running to greet the couple as if they were lifelong friends returning from the "war" in Grenada. As she sloppily hugged them, she spilled her drink on Monroe.

"I'm so sorry!" She patted down his shirt with a cocktail napkin. "At least it was only Chardie."

"Chardie?" asked Monroe.

"Chardonnay, silly."

Maddie clapped her hands. "That's so cool; I've never heard that one. Wait, where are my manners? This is Mon—"

"He's Monroe. I brought him in when Jacks dropped him off."

"Thank so much for doing that, Jaia," she said.

Jaia wadded up the wet napkin and tossed it into a corner. "Maddie, you didn't tell me that your friend's so cute."

Maddie didn't like where this was going. She shuddered at the thought of Demi Moore leading her man down the abyss in the dark. "Yes," she said with a smile, "my *boyfriend* is cute, isn't he?"

Jaia ignored that. "Hey, Maddie, I need to powder my nose. Why don't you come with me?"

"Huh?"

"To the ladies' room down the hall. I need to go." Instead of pointing to her bladder, she pointed to her nose.

Before Maddie had a chance to answer, she took her by the hand and dragged her down the hall.

Alone now, Monroe surveyed the room. There were a lot of cool-looking people, but also a few mullet-heads and aging hippie types. He noticed a score of trendies in spiky, multicolored hair standing at the periphery of the crowded room, dressed like they could've been extras in the original *Blade Runner*.

A sexy, red-haired replicant came up to him and asked what he wanted.

"Come again?"

"To drink," she added.

He said a gin and tonic would be good, and she took off to get it. He hadn't expected wait-service.

Then he waited for a long, long time, fidgeting, and wishing to God that he had his iPhone so he could twiddle his thumbs on some Angry Birds. He thought of Maddie and that crazy Rory Weedham, he thought of his life in the 21st century from his earliest memories of toddlerhood, to his grade school and high school years, his time at UCLA, and all his past relationships. Then he thought of the pros (none) and cons of supply-side economics, the 1986 immigration amnesty act, and finally about his first pet as a child, a speckled hamster named Susan. Without a smartphone he felt like he'd thought every thought a human could think in their lifetime.

Exactly four minutes later, the replicant arrived with his g&t. He sipped it—yuck!— too much g and not enough t. And where was the frickin' olive?

He turned to the guy next to him, a black-and-green haired young gentleman whose bangs flipped down to obscure his right eye. "This drink's too strong for me" said Monroe, "Do you want it?"

The guy furrowed his one visible brow. "Dude, I just saw you drink out of it! Do I look like I want AIDS?"

Monroe hated to come off as a know-it-all, but come the fuck on. "Dude, even if I had AIDS..." Monroe stopped, noticing the people around him clearing away. He lowered his voice. "You can't get it from saliva."

"Like you would know!" The one-eyed dunce made a beeline across the room.

Somewhere in the already-loud hotel room, someone was yelling to get everyone's attention. Then there was a BOOM! Chips of plaster rained down from the ceiling. Everyone stopped what they were doing. Monroe looked over and saw a curly-haired dwarf in shades jumping up on the bed and waving a smoking pistol. Not a proverbial one, but the real thing.

"Now that I have your attention," said the gun-toting spectacle, "I want you all to hear the soon-to-be-released Richard and the Ramirez's album produced by yours truly."

"Tell me when, Philly," a big-haired blonde said, her hand on the arm of a portable record turntable.

Phil gave her the signal, and she put it on. "Crank the tunes!" he ordered.

Monroe covered his ears. He wasn't interested in some punk-ass band screaming corny shit about Satan and his sneakers. He looked around for a break in the seemingly transfixed crowd to find the exit.

Though he worried that Maddie and Jaia wouldn't find him if he left, he figured the room was already so maxed out they wouldn't have gotten in anyway. Monroe navigated his way through the mass of legs and crotches like Joe Montana running a quarterback sneak around of The Refrigerator in some crazy maze, like that one from his favorite 80s horror movie, *The Shining*. At last, he reached the door.

He felt a SWOOSH go right past him and heard the crack of wood as Phil discharged a bullet in the door frame, just inches away from him.

The music stopped.

"Where in the name of Chevy-Fucking-Chase do you think you're going?!" he shouted at Monroe, who stood stiff as steel against the door. "Nobody leaves until the album is through!"

The crowd turned to look at the legendary producer's object of rage.

Monroe's heart pounded. Sweat oozed out of every pore in his body. He wished he'd drunk the gin he'd given to that ignorant clown.

"That's the guy who tried to give me AIDS!" cried a voice in the back.

"The dude's got AIDS!" yelled someone in front, a hulking guy in a Boy George getup.

The crowd starting screaming.

Surprisingly, it was Richard Ramirez to Monroe's rescue. "Phil, let that loser go," he pleaded. "We don't need any AIDS-bags in here."

Phil cleared his throat. "Okay then, the AIDS-bag goes." He shot the ceiling again to emphasize his point. "I mean *now!*"

Monroe high-tailed it out before the soon-to-be murderous producer had time to aim his pistol at him again.

He ran down a dark hallway. It was definitely not the place he'd come in from. He stumbled on an old steam pipe, barely avoiding hitting someone concealed in the shadows.

It was Jaia.

"Hey," she said, deftly stepping aside. When she turned her head, he realized she had one of those miner lights on her head, which glared into his face. "What are you doing here?"

"It's a long story," he said, squinting. He dusted off his pants. "Where's Maddie?"

"She's in the ladies' room with the Peruvian girls. It might take a while."

"Why?"

"Nose candy, silly."

"Why aren't you in there, too?"

"I've had more than enough, thank you very much. But I don't have time to talk. I need to help you get me out of here. Quick!"

"What's going on?"

"I'll tell you later." She grabbed his hand, and they ran.

While trying to avoid the slalom course of steam pipes, cables, and dead rats, she explained that she'd been on the fourth-floor communal bathroom doing lines with a Columbian when he made a move on her and she had to fend him off. She reached for a glass soap dispenser by the sink and threw it.

The bottle, she told him, found its mark—the bad guy's forehead—and shattered to pieces. It turned out that the dispenser was filled with uncut cocaine, which scattered like a Texas cyclone throughout the bathroom before descending into a fog and into the nearest toilet. As the dude pulled the bloody shards from his brow, he said worked for the Escobar family and that she just destroyed ten grand worth of blow. She told Monroe that she ran out of there as fast as she could. As they conversed more, he found that not only was Jaia's knowledge of cinema extensive, she was totally articulate in analyzing important films. And she hated TV, she said.

That was okay with Monroe. Sure, sometimes could get into the kitsch of an old *Saved by the Bell* episode, but, unlike Maddie, he didn't dig 1980s shows or the commercials. But movies, that was different. In his excitement, he told her how he'd seen *Rain Man* about a dozen times in college. Jaia looked confused until he realized that the film wouldn't come out for another five years. He changed the topic to Dustin Hoffman in *Tootsie* and they both had a laugh. (In her case, a nervous laugh, since she feared the cartel dude could be lurking in the vicinity.)

Then they heard footsteps—she couldn't afford to wait to see who it could be, so Jaia grabbed Monroe, telling him to follow her.

They came to a viaduct ahead of them. "Come on," she said, getting ready to climb in.

Monroe halted. "We don't even know where this goes."

"I'm pretty sure this'll take us down to the service entrance."

"How do you know?"

She told him that she knew where the sewer lines crossed in most pre-War buildings in L.A. She told him that she had once wanted to be an engineer but now she wasn't so sure, and how she was thinking of deferring a year before attending MIT in the fall.

"MIT, huh? You must be brilliant."

"If I were," she laughed, her braces gleaming beneath the beam of her headlamp, "I wouldn't be climbing into a sewer pipe."

Only one at a time could fit, so since it was her idea, Jaia went first. They crawled through a gopher-like warren of tunnels lit by only by her miner's beam until they found the door she was looking for.

She jiggled the knob. "It's locked." She reached up into her hair. "Damn, my bobby pin must have fallen out. Wait, I think we can find another way." She turned around.

Monroe used his hands to shield his eyes from the glare of her headlamp. "Where'd you get that thing, anyway? Please tell me you don't bring miner's lights whenever you go out on the town." Secretly, Monroe was concerned he'd somehow missed a cool '80s fashion factoid in all his previous research.

"Ha! No. It was one of the things that fell out of Richard's backpack when he was running to talk to Philly. Jacks loves old funky stuff like that, so I took it. Little did I know how it would come in handy."

"What else did he have in his backpack?"

"Weird stuff. Duct tape, a rope, garbage bag ties..."

Suddenly, Monroe realized what Maddie was about to tell him when he first arrived at the party. It was the '80's most infamous serial killer, aka, The Night Stalker. "Oh, God! He's gonna kill. We gotta go back to get Maddie, and save her from Richard!"

"Monroe, don't wig out. Besides, I can't go back there, what with Escobar's bitch looking for me."

"But I can't find my way back without you!"

"Yeah, but—"

Suddenly, a THWUMP came from outside the door. Someone was hacking away at the metal door. Another big hit, and they got a glimpse of an ax blade stuck in the doorjamb. They saw the blade see-saw as the ax's owner tried to extricate it.

"This is just like *The Shining*!" Monroe cried.

They didn't wait to see how that played out. "Follow me," she whispered and slipped through another, smaller tube. He needed no further prodding. He squeezed in and crawled through after her.

## 6. [slw]

Maddie couldn't make heads or tails of what those Peruvian girls were saying, except that they were hoping they could get Phil Spector to produce their album. Which reminded Maddie that she still needed to find a Yellow Pages so she could call up those future victims to warn them. She should also call Dustin Hoffman and Warren Beatty to warn them about *Ishtar*, she thought.

As she skipped down the hallway—uncut '80s cocaine gave quite the kick!—Maddie realized she had no idea where Jaia had gone. The last time she saw the girl, she'd been sucking up to some swarthy drug dealer. *Maybe I'm better off without her, even if she does have some bitchin' accessories.*

Maddie made her way back to the party just as the last track on the second side of the upcoming Richard and the Ramirez's LP was winding down. She noticed a whiff of gunpowder competing with the smells of perfume, hairspray, pot, and gin-puke. Then she noticed that Monroe was not in the room.

She wended her way through the crowd and to the window to see if she could spot him outside. All she saw in the breaking dawn were a few domicile-challenged individuals gathered around a trashcan fire, parked cars, and a huge billboard for Marlboro cigarettes.

*I can't believe they actually advertised cancer-sticks to the public!*

She turned, then surveyed the room. Unless he was in the can, Monroe wasn't here. The crowd had thinned out some, which may also have something to do with the smell of gunpowder, she surmised. Philly was standing on the bed, his pistol holstered, clearly engrossed in the album. Richard was sitting on the edge of the bed, cleaning under his fingernails with the blade of a small pocketknife.

The final song faded, and Phil began jumping up and down. "Again, again!" he commanded.

Maddie saw a big-haired blonde stationed by a portable record player. "Gnarly," she said, beaming at the diminutive producer. She plucked the demo from the turntable, flipped it over, and played it from track one, side one.

"This shit's the musical equivalent of a banged funny bone," someone whispered in her ear.

Maddie stepped back and said, "Oh, hey. You're the drummer, aren't you?"

The pockmarked punk-guy grinned and nodded. "Ricardo." He shook her hand. "Yeah, I am, but I don't really know how to play."

*You don't say*, Maddie thought. "How'd you wind up in a band, then?"

"Oh, you know," he shrugged, frowning. "I'm into devil worship."

"Makes sense," Maddie said agreeably. "But not really-really, right? I mean… you're not like Richard, are you?"

"How so?"

"Well… you've never thought about killing people, have you?"

"Of course I have. What's the point of Satanism without human sacrifices?"

Maddie took a few steps away from the drummer. "Hey, have you seen my boyfriend lately? His name is Monroe and he's got this cool Flock of Seagulls haircut."

Richard stood up, pocketed his knife, and approached Maddie. "You mean the AIDS-bag? We got rid of him."

"Got rid of?" Maddie echoed. "What do you mean, 'got rid of'? And AIDS? Monroe doesn't have AIDS."

"Whatever," Richard shrugged. Then he took Maddie by the elbow. "I want to show you something. Come over here, it's in my backpack." The second song on the LP was now playing. It started with a fusillade of jangled dissonance, then got worse. Richard grinned. "Oh, this is my favorite—*Dyin' After Midnight*. You like it?"

"Umm," Maddie demurred. "Look, much as I'd like to hear your album again and see your rape-kit, I've gotta go find my boyfriend."

The budding serial killer gripped Maddie's upper arm painfully hard. "You're not going anywhere, you blue-haired bitch."

Just then, Phil jumped down from the sagging bed. His short legs made surprisingly fast tracks, and the next thing Maddie knew, he was nose-to-collarbone with Richard. "Much as I hate to see a ripe young female leave my party, I think you should unhand her, Ramirez."

Richard tightened his grip, and Maddie squeaked in pain.

The drummer ambled off, presumably in search of a more chill scene, leaving Maddie more or less alone with the two volatile men.

Without losing his grip on Maddie, Richard pulled his knife and poised the blade just shy of Phil's jugular. While she couldn't see his eyes very well behind the dark shades, Maddie could tell they were blazing with righteous indignation.

"So, this is how it's gonna be, huh? After all I did for you and your shitty band?"

"Oh, we're shitty now, are we?" Richard seethed through clenched, stained teeth. "Well, I think your Wall of Sound is nothing but overproduced hype!"

Phil unholstered his pistol and brandished it. "Say that again, you two-bit hack. You're no Bill Medley, and you couldn't even *touch* The Ronettes! Not like I did," he smirked.

Finally, Richard let Maddie go. "Oh, yeah?" he retorted.

"Yeah!" Phil barked.

As the two men began to circle each other and shake their bodies just like the dancers in Pat Benatar's *Hell is for Children* music video, the partygoers gathered to watch the fracas. Maddie wanted desperately to flee the room, grab Monroe, and go, but she couldn't because she was trapped between the barred window and the murderous duo.

Phil pointed his gun at the ceiling, then fired.

"Hey, stop that!" someone from the fifth floor shouted.

Phil fired again.

Maddie's ears rang, and she felt weak. She watched in mute horror as Richard jabbed at Phil's soft belly, drawing blood.

The music man put his hand to his midsection, then stared in disbelief at the blood on his hand. "You son of a bitch," he muttered, bringing his weapon down and pointing it at Richard's head. "Try that again."

Richard laughed, low and menacing. "Hail Satan!" he said, then skewered the producer's jugular notch, doing a deadly tracheotomy.

As Phil tried to curb the flow of blood with his free hand, he pressed the pistol between Richard's eyes and fired. Instantly, brain matter blew out from the back of the punker's head as his skull shattered and flew in shards across the room.

Those within range stumbled back. "Ugh, barf me out!" shouted the man in the Boy George getup, swiping a chunk of viscera from his headband.

Maddie watched, wide-eyed, as the two men crumpled to the floor in gory heaps. The metallic smell of gunpowder and blood made her guts roil. She turned and tried desperately to open the window—she felt the need to leave now, by any means necessary. Much to her dismay, the window was nailed shut.

Then she saw it. The Marlboro billboard had changed to an ad for *Bill and Ted's Excellent Adventure*. "Opens Friday, August 19, 1983," read the words in Amiga-style typeface at the bottom. "Nineteen-eighty-three?" Maddie breathed. "No... *Bill and Ted's Excellent Adventure* doesn't come out until '87. What the...?"

*Oh, fuck,* she thought. *I caused this! I made a paradox that killed Phil Spector and Richard Ramirez. Sure, I saved a ton of lives, but look at that!* She squinted at the 15-foot-tall image of an actor who should have been Keanu Reeves. *I ruined Keanu's career!* The other guy was still on the poster, but now he was flanked by Gary Coleman.

Maddie realized she had to get out. Not just out of the seedy hotel room, but out of the 1980s entirely.

Rory had been right: she couldn't hack it. Not only were there crazed killers coming out of the wood-paneling, everyone was so politically incorrect and misogynistic. The hairspray was aerosol, the gum had cancerous red dye in it, and worst of all, there was no Starbucks. She could really, really use a double ristretto venti half-soy nonfat decaf organic chocolate brownie iced vanilla double-shot gingerbread Frappuccino extra hot with foam whipped cream upside down double blended with Stevia-in-the-raw, right about now.

Maddie looked at the gaping crowd, and for once she was glad the iPhone hadn't been invented yet. She could imagine the Insta stories she'd otherwise be tagged in, standing over the dead bodies of Spector and Ramirez. She'd be canceled for sure.

She took a deep breath and stepped over the bodies. No one stopped her from leaving, but Ricardo, the Ramirez's drummer, did give her a dirty look while quickly swiping his index finger across his throat.

7. [dgs]

Maddie managed to find her way outside the grungy hotel without attracting too much attention. Somewhere along the way, a woman with Cyndi Lauper hair told Maddie that she'd seen someone in a Flock of Seagulls hairdo hitch a ride with a Jon Bon Jovi lookalike. She assumed that meant that Monroe must've gotten a ride back to the motel. What she didn't realize was, 'Roe wasn't the only guy there with the Flock of Seagulls look.

As Maddie ventured outside and into the alley, she realized she wasn't out of the woods yet. Phil's friend, the jerk with the Boy George fetish, was standing with a foot planted on his faded yellow Gremlin, smoking a clove cigarette. He smiled at her like he was posing for Warhol's *Interview* magazine and said, "Looks like you could use a ride."

Maddie looked away. The Peruvian sisters she'd been tooting in the bathroom with had warned her about a "George Chico" who was *no es bueno.*

"I'm good."

"What does that mean?"

*Oh God, not another idiot,* she thought. "I mean, I don't need a ride." Knowing that she couldn't just call for an Uber, she looked around for a cab. This wasn't the hip DTLA Monroe had taken her to just last week. This place smelled less of Charles Bukowski wannabes in manbuns sipping craft scotch, and more like crack and feces. The only cars she saw were parked, but their chasses were bouncing, most likely from various paid activities of the ladies and gentlemen of the night. People slept all over the sidewalks, and some even on the streets themselves. She was shocked to see even more homeless people than the 2020s.

The *no es bueno* Boy George looked sketchy, but the crazies on the streets looked even worse. She told him that she'd take him up on the car ride offer so long as he kept his hands to himself. He agreed to take her, adding that Hollywood was on his way, and that he dated prettier girls, so no, there wouldn't be any monkey business.

Maddie sighed, realizing that pre-Me Too, guys would make comments—both good and bad—about a woman's appearance without a second thought.

She hesitated but got into his Gremlin. They took off. She desperately wished she'd had her iPhone so she could pretend to swipe and not have to talk to this jerk. The guy started babbling about Reeboks, *E.T.*, and *Dynasty* until she turned up the dial and cranked *I'll Tumble 4 Ya* on his 8-track to muffle his noise. She couldn't wait to get back to the motel, though she wasn't looking forward to admitting to Monroe that she was wrong: the '80s sucked. Even worse, she knew it was too late to catch a flight to New

York plead with Rory to get the fuck out of this hellish decade.

Bad Boy George dropped her off in front of the dilapidated motel without a backward glance.

She went to her room. There was no sign of Monroe. She peered out the window to see the lights off in the motel office. Where was Jaia, and where was her 'Roe?

...

They were still ambling through the dark bowels of the Cecil Hotel, trying to stay one step ahead of the drug dealer and the guy with the ax. Jaia led Monroe through smaller and smaller tunnels until they finally found an opening: a door leading to a ladder, which led them to the roof.

Once there, Monroe looked at the city skyline, an unimpressive jumble of low buildings that would one day be cleared for skyscrapers.

The girl with Cyndi Lauper hair was there. She was freebasing coke with some preppy-looking dick with frosted hair and a pink Izod shirt. The dick turned to look at Jaia and Monroe, breaking his drug-imbibing concentration and thereby setting his hair on fire. The faux Cyndi dumped a drink on his head and put out the flames.

Monroe asked the two if they'd seen Maddie. The Lauperette said she'd seen a girl who matched the description of Mads driving off with a Boy George. Before Monroe could press the girl for more details, she passed out.

The burnt-hair preppy dick asked them if they'd seen his ax. "It's not a guitar." He started to describe it. "You know, a tool with a wooden handle and a sharp blade.

"We know what an ax looks like," said Jaia.

"Looks like you're sitting on it," said Monroe, pointing to a blade that looked like it was wedging into the guy's cross-legged ass.

Preppy dick looked down but was unfazed. "Guess you're right," he said with a glassy-eyed smile. Apropos of nothing, the guy told them that he and his girl had gone out for a smoke downstairs but had been locked out. He said he'd used the fire ax to break open the door to the service entrance to get back to the roof.

Jaia and Monroe breathed a sigh of relief. The guy looked too wasted to be an effective ax murderer. Anyway, he looked more like a future embezzler than a killer.

Just then, the sound of a pan flute doodling wafted from the stairwell.

"Oh no!" exclaimed Jaia as she clutched Monroe tightly, "It's probably that Escobar dude!"

As the pan flute tooted ever closer, Monroe instinctively got in front of Jaia to protect her. He wasn't about to let someone, even some powerful drug kingpin, harm this poor girl.

Luckily, he didn't have to defend her. The kingpin came out on the roof with the Peruvian girls, singing and dancing to what Monroe believed to be either a classic narco-ballad or a Wall of Voodoo song. They looked like they were high as kites, and when they caught a glimpse of Jaia, they greeted her like a long-lost war buddy. Mr. Escobar, or whoever he really was, showed everyone the cuts on his forehead and even thanked Jaia for "knocking some sense" into his *cabeza*.

Then the Peruvian sisters started singing something even more dark and tuneless. Though they were warbling in Spanish, Jaia immediately knew they were riffing on *Nuclear Brain Dance*, Rory Weedham's first hit.

To Monroe's surprise, Jaia did a cartwheel on the roof and joined in on the song, singing the English lyrics.

Monroe was impressed. "Hey, we're going to see Weedham at the Troubadour tomorrow night; wanna come?" he asked her.

"I wish! It's been sold out for months!"

Sold out? That was news to him. How was he going to get in the club so that Rory could take him and Maddie back to the 21st century? Of course, that was assuming that Maddie would agree to go back with him. He was irritated at her flightiness ever since they'd been in the 1980s, and he wondered whether she'd plead with Rory to stay. Monroe had been dismayed that Maddie would go to the bathroom to do blow. Sure, Jaia had done it, but did people really know in 1983 that this shit was bad news? He thought Maddie had been acting douchey, and that made him worry about her possible future acts of douchebaggery.

Monroe wasn't just having second thoughts about Maddie, but also about going back to the 21st century. He had to admit that, once he got over all the retro-shock, he kind of liked 1983. He'd read in the *Herald Examiner* back at the motel that the average one-bedroom place in Los Angeles rented for an "obscenely high" $308 per month. He didn't mind a little crime and smog for those prices. Plus, if he stayed back in time, he'd never have to pay off his student loans. Even though a lot of people here were kind of dull—and he resolved to punch the next idiot who told him to "wake up and smell the coffee" —at least they talked to each other rather than engaging in parallel play with their phones.

And then there was his concern for Jaia. He didn't want to leave her to destroy her life studying something she hated at MIT, or to go to more murderous coke parties. Or she might stay working at the motel for her dad, toiling away with a man she'd described as bitter and depressed, a man who hated himself for unwittingly giving his wife a deadly pill. (When they were still in chambers of the Cecil Hotel, she'd explained, with barely-controlled tears, that her mother had been one of the victims in the Tylenol murders back in Chicago, and that they had moved out West to escape the memories.)

The Peruvian sisters and their drug dealer stopped dancing to take a blow-break. As the partyers re-filled their nostrils with white powder, Monroe and Jaia said their goodbyes and left.

Now that they no longer feared for their lives, they decided to leave via the normal route. The door from the rooftop back inside was indeed secured, just like the burnt-haired preppy had said, but Jaia took out a Diner's Club card and jimmied the lock. They climbed downstairs and exited the building through the zigs and zags they'd used to get in.

They walked along the dark streets of boxy cars with smashed-in windows until finding Jaia's VW which, happily for them, had no windows to smash.

They got in and drove to the 405 heading west. After a couple of miles, though, their stomachs started growling, so she exited the freeway in search of eats.

If this was in "his day," thought Monroe, he would've suggested one of those tasty 24-hour taco trucks in East Hollywood, but in here in 1983 he knew that place was off-limits unless you carried an Uzi. And, of course, they couldn't just head back to the motel and place a DoorDash order. He comforted himself with the thought that at least whatever they found to eat wouldn't have kale in it.

They found the only thing open—a 7/11—and parked. But Monroe was hesitant to go in. He'd seen the convenience store robbery scene in *Fast Times at Ridgemont High* about a thousand times. But Jaia went inside before he even had a chance to voice his reservations, so he followed her. She immediately found her snack: Beer Nuts. Monroe scoured the aisles, unable to decide between Zingers and Pop Rocks. If this 7/11 was any indication, he thought, convenience stores hadn't changed much. Sure, the coffee was served in Styrofoam and the place was cash-only, but except for the multitude of magazines for sale, he could be in any AM/PM store in the 2020s.

They walked by newspapers with headlines screaming crime, drugs, and the recession. A *Newsweek* cover article questioned whether continued high unemployment would tank President Reagan's poll numbers even more.

He wondered whether he should tell Jaia about his past, or rather, about the future. He could've elaborated about the Black Monday stock market crash that would follow. Instead he just said, "Well, that's my guess, anyway."

They paid the cashier a buck, told him to keep the change, and walked out. Just in time, too. As they got back in the car, they saw a sullen-looking dude with a sunburned face, dolphin shorts, and a murderous mullet walk in with a handgun.

Without waiting to put on their seat belts, they sped off toward Fairfax, just as the sun was coming up. A church bell rang somewhere in the distance. It was Sunday. By midnight tonight, Monroe thought with a twinge of sadness, he'd be with Rory floating his way back to the 2020s.

The light turned red. Monroe looked at Jaia.

Jaia looked at Monroe.

They kissed.

Then came the honking. The light had turned green.

She smiled at him and floored the pedal. "Where to now?"

8. [slw]

Maddie was just falling asleep in the tiny motel room when she heard something moving. It was the doorknob. She sat up, squinting. It was turning, this way and that. Someone was trying to get in! Her heart pounded. What if it was one of the Ramirez's trying to exact revenge for her part—unwitting though it may have been—in the deadly gun-vs-knife fight? Or, more likely, it was Bad Boy George. He'd dropped her off without a backward glance, but who was to say he hadn't changed his mind about her level of prettiness?

She let out her breath. *Duh.* It was Monroe, who'd probably forgotten his key. She got up and went to the door. There was no Ring surveillance, not even a no-tech peephole, so she called out, "Monroe? Is that you?"

"No," came a male voice in reply. "It's Jacks... with the facts. And with an order from Jack-in-the-Box. I thought you might be hungry."

*Jacks?* Oh, yeah, Maddie remembered: Jaia's brother, who'd dropped Monroe off at The Cecil. She started to turn the knob, then stopped. How would she know it's really him? They'd never actually met.

"Describe my boyfriend," she called through the flimsy, hollow-core door.

"Total dweeb. Flock of Seagulls hair."

"Just a sec," Maddie said, reaching for her jeans. She pulled them on, then opened the door. "Hi," she said. "Where's Monroe?"

Jacks walked in, a greasy bag of fast food in one hand. "Probably with Jaia. I don't know. Are you hungry?" He dumped the contents of the bag on the rickety card table, and the small room filled with the smell of pressed hash brown wedges and heatlamp-dried breakfast sandwiches.

Maddie was too hungry to care—she hadn't eaten since the 2020s. They sat at the table and wolfed the food down.

"Thanks," Maddie said, feeling much better. But she was still worried about Monroe. What if he never came back and left her stranded in 1983? She got up, then turned on the TV. "I hope you don't mind," she said to Jacks. "I need to make sure I'm not on the news."

Jacks smiled. "Right. Are you some sort of fugitive? We don't have insurance for police shootouts. Actually," he said conspiratorially, "we don't have insurance for anything."

Once the tube warmed up, the TV had sound and picture. The lead story was indeed about the brutal death of "revered music producer" Phil Spector and how one of his proteges, whose name was being withheld, had murdered him. *So, I really did alter the course of history*. She wondered what—aside from the *Bill and Ted's Excellent Adventure* jumble—negative repercussions there might be. As she watched the fawning tribute to Spector, she was relieved to see that there was no mention of her at all.

She looked over at Jacks, who was watching the news with disinterest. He didn't say anything, so Maddie had to assume that Monroe hadn't mentioned anything to Jacks about the time-travel thing. "Well," she said, "thanks for bringing breakfast. How much do I owe you?"

He stood. "Nothing, sweet-cheeks. It's on the house." Then he went to the door and let himself out.

Maddie decided to lay low until Monroe came back. Not only was she exhausted from last night's awful adventure and worried about running into a Ramirez or Bad Boy George, but she also had a lot of thinking to do.

She couldn't relax, thanks to the second wave of cocaine coursing through her system, but she did lie down. She'd already made up her mind to go back to the 2020s, with or without 'Roe. There was just too much bloodshed and spandex in the '80s. She didn't think she could even bear to be a member of The Raddies anymore—if she was lucky enough to get back unscathed.

There had to be a way to welch on the bet—the last thing she wanted to do was sleep with Rory Weedham. His music was cool and all, but he was old enough to be her grandpa. *Wait. There could be a loophole*, she thought. *Rory did mention that he's younger in 1983. I could do it here, before going home. But he hasn't fixed his teeth yet. Hm.* She weighed the pros and cons, and finally fell asleep.

She woke up several hours later. She glanced at the clock on the nightstand and saw that it was 7 p.m. She'd slept through the whole day. She sat up and looked around the room. No sign of Monroe.

She got cleaned up, finger-combed her hair, double-checked her pockets for the money—the balance was still there—then went to the clerk's office to turn in her key and pay up for the extra hours. The grumpy old man was there, and when Maddie asked if Jaia or Jacks was in, he just shook his head and asked her if she needed her penny in change. She'd seen *Somewhere in Time* enough times to know that was a bad idea, so she told him to keep it.

The sun was low in the sky, but since it was summer, it would be another couple of hours till total darkness, which made Maddie feel somewhat safer about walking to The Troubadour alone. She prayed that Monroe would meet her there. If he didn't, she couldn't guess what might happen. Then an even more disturbing thought came to her:

What if Rory didn't show up? She couldn't bear to be forced to live in a world where Gary Coleman was Theodore "Ted" Logan, sexism ran rampant, and the selfie stick didn't exist yet.

When she reached The Troubadour, she was both relieved and anxious. The marquee bore Rory Weedham's name as the main event, but the opening act listed below was billed as: The Ramirez's Minus Richard. *Shit*, she thought. That look the drummer had given her as she was leaving the hotel room came back to her like a scene from a rewound videotape.

The line stretched down the block. Maddie had to figure out what to do. Rory had given them money, but no tickets. He'd made it all seem so easy, but judging from the size of the crowd, she couldn't just waltz in and ask to see the headliner. She went to the start of the line and saw a paper sign tacked to a station. It read: *Sold out! Overflow ticket line starts here.*

She turned, and bumped into someone. "Sorry," she muttered.

"I'm not," came the reply. "What luck running into you here."

Maddie looked up and into the face of The Ramirez's drummer. "Damn," she muttered.

"Damn right," he smirked, pinching the back of her neck between his thumb and fingers, then firmly forcing her through the front door of the club. "She's with me," the drummer said to a bouncer, then herded Maddie across the empty floor and to the backstage area.

The bassist was sitting on a folding chair smoking a cigarette. He came to full attention when he saw Maddie. "Whoa, where'd you find the bitch?" he asked his bandmate.

"She practically fell into my lap," said the drummer, letting go of Maddie's neck but taking a hold of her wrists.

"Satan always provides," said the bassist. "Should we waste her now, or sacrifice her onstage?"

Ricardo pondered this for a moment. "I like your sense of showmanship, Rickie, but this is our first time playing as a duo, so fitting a brutal bloodletting into the act could be tricky. Also, we're only opening. We shouldn't steal Weedham's thunder."

"Good points," said the bassist agreeably, standing up. He approached Maddie, then gave her a good, long look. His super-sprayed claw bangs almost covered the pentagram he'd carved into the middle of his forehead. "We kill her now."

The drummer half-walked, half-pushed Maddie toward what looked to be a clothes closet. The bassist followed.

"No!" Maddie yelled, planting her feet. "Help! Help me! I'm being sacrificed by 1980s

Satanists!" There was no response, and Ricardo didn't loosen his grip. She caught the sound of Rickie unsheathing a knife. Then she remembered the month and the year. "The McMartins are here! Help!"

The closet door opened, and Maddie found herself face-to-face-to-face with Monroe and Jaia. Clearly the two had been making out, as they hastily straightened their clothes and turned bright red when they saw her. But Maddie was too scared to be mad at them right now. "Help!" she repeated.

Monroe pulled Maddie free from Ricardo, while Jaia rushed at the assailants. The aspiring MIT student took the travel-sized Aqua Net from her fanny pack and let The Ramirez's have it right in the eyes with a blast of aerosol-propelled spray.

"Bloody hell!" someone yelled. "This is bollocks!"

Now there was another man in the hairspray fray.

It was Rory Weedham, who'd entered the kerfuffle quite by accident when he stumbled into the dressing room looking for his pre-show bottle of Jim Beam whiskey. He was stooped over, frantically rubbing his eyes.

"Rory!" Maddie cried, rushing to him. She threw her arms around the sexy, now young, keytar player. "I'm so glad to see you!"

Rory blinked at her without recognition.

Jaia was still chasing The Ramirez's around the dressing room with her can of Aqua Net.

Monroe just stood there, gawping stupidly.

Maddie had to act fast. She grabbed Rory by his rainbow suspenders and pulled him into the closet with her. She tugged the door shut, tore her shirt open, and unzipped her jeans.

"You American birds are so forward," Rory grinned, showing off a missing eyetooth. His eyes were red and teary, but he was far from impaired. He slipped his suspenders free and dropped trou.

"Oh, Rory," Maddie sighed as the rock star did what rock stars do when they find themselves shut inside backstage closets with young blue-haired women.

"Oh, Maddie," he replied.

"You remember me?" she moaned. "Thank God. Please take me back to the 21st century, Rory. You were right—I can't last another second in the '80s!"

"I can't last another second, either," he grunted, finishing their quickie. He stepped back, pulled his pants up, then helped Maddie with her clothes. "I was hoping you'd lose that bet, dearie." He gave her a tender kiss. "But you can't leave the '80s just yet. I've got a show to do. I never disappoint my fans."

Maddie pondered this. She'd hoped that the closet floor would just open up and send them down (up?) the chute that led back to Rory's 2020s immaculate white den. Then again, she shouldn't leave without 'Roe. That would be rude, even if he was cheating on her with a cocaine-snorting, VW Thing driving, motel clerk.

She realized she wasn't hearing anything outside the door. She reached over and turned the knob.

Rory pushed the door open, and they both looked out into the dressing room.

It was empty of people.

9. [dgs]

Rory went to the illuminated mirror and took a seat. The first thing he did was to drop some Visine into his red, irritated eyes. Then he reached into the drawer and pulled out a makeup kit.

"Back in the day," he told Maddie, "uh, I mean now, I'd have a girl like you do my makeup for me."

"A girl like me?" She crossed her arms.

"You know, a tour girl or a wing-fling. I mean, that's what everyone here should think. So, to make you look like legit groupie, here—take this."  He handed her some foundation to get started.

She rolled her eyes but took the cosmetics anyway. *Anything to get back home*, she told herself. Under his direction, she gave him his whole stage look, with makeup heavy enough to entomb The Cure and all their instruments, too. He transformed himself into some kind of androgynous love-child of Annie Lennox and Simon Le Bon, with a dash of pre-child-molesting Gary Glitter thrown into the mix.

As they appraised Rory's new look, the door swung open behind them.

In walked a middle-aged guy with a pirate patch and graying ponytail. "Where the fuck is your band?" he barked at Rory.

"Like I told you before, the ladies will be onstage at show time," Rory said. "Chillax, mate, these chicks are punctual."

"They better be, 'cause showtime's in 30 fuckin' minutes!" the ponytailer said. "Jesus. *Rhys* I could handle, *Russell Aquarius* I could handle. But you?!" He exited, slamming the door so hard, the flimsy walls rattled.

Rory put his head in his hands. "Asshole."

"Who is he?" asked Maddie.

"My manager."

"What's this about 'the ladies'? I don't remember you having an all-girl band."

"You will now." He winked at her. "Mark my words, when we get back home there'll be a new entry on Wikipedia. And these girls can rock!"

"How often have you been here—I mean, back in time?"

"I go back at least once or twice a year." The Englishman smiled his post-war, rotted-tooth grin. "Coke, women, and song. What could be better?"

The door flew open again. "I caught these two outside your door," Rory's manager said, dragging Monroe and Jaia into view.

"It's cool, Sid," said Rory, "Let them in."

Rory turned to Jaia. "Wait, are you my new drummer?"

She looked at Rory in awe. "No, but... I could learn."

Rory narrowed his eyes. "Hold on! You're the one who sprayed me in the face!"

"I'm sorry, Mr. Weedham," she said. "I was trying to get The Ramirez's."

"My opening act? Why?"

"They're Satanists and probably murderers, too," Maddie supplied.

Rory smirked. "So?"

"Never mind all that," interjected Monroe. "I need to talk to you guys about Jaia and me."

"I get it," said Maddie. "I'm cool with it."

"You are? Great, so... actually, I've decided that I want to stay here with her."

"Hold on," said Rory, "Nobody said anything about you getting to stay."

"But, Mr. Weedham," said Jaia, "I like Monroe. If he has to go, please, then take me with you guys."

"If your new bird comes with you," Rory told Monroe, "She'll be 40 years older. Grey-haired, probably plump, maybe even a QAnon nutcase."

"Well, I don't care," said Monroe.

"Actually," said Jaia, "I kind of do. Old age is grody. Can't Monroe just stay here with me?"

"Please?" pleaded Monroe. "From what I've seen so far, the '80s needs a lot of work. If I stay, maybe I can get involved in some do-gooder stuff and try and make a difference around here, you know?"

Rory let out a mirthless laugh. "Good luck with that, mate. I've been trying for years to change the past. I mean, I once even trained John Hinkley to shoot better and finish the job, but none of that shit did any good. Each time, that old windbag Reagan survived."

Sid, who'd been standing by quietly, handed Rory a packet labeled: *Pre-show Toot.* Then he turned to the other three and sternly said, "Now the rest of you, skedaddle!"

Rory pulled out his compact mirror and a razor blade. "See you guys after the show. Siddie, make sure they have tickets and backstage passes."

Sid grumbled, reaching into his back pocket. He thrust the goods at the trio, and they each took a lanyard. "Now, you kids, va-fucking-moose. And Weedham, don't ever call me Siddie again."

The kids left with their stage passes, and they all promised to meet after the show.

Maddie showed her pass to bouncer and stepped toward the standing room only area part of the club, followed by Jaia and Monroe.

They got there just as The Ramirez's Minus Richard were being booed off the stage.

*Red Skies at Night* started booming through the P.A. while the roadies set up for Rory. Maddie loved The Fixx, at least their earlier music, but it was boring just standing around without a smartphone. Among other things, she wanted so bad to Google whether *One Thing Leads to Another* had come out yet. She turned and looked at the people around her. They were just talking with each other or staring into space, perhaps lost in thought. *How did people live this? Like animals!*

Finally, the lights dimmed around them and the audience shuffled closer to the dark stage. The excitement was palpable.

Synthesizers glissed up and down the scale, the bass guitarist tuned up, and next came the boom-boom boom-boom four-on-the-floor kick drum. With every bounce of the echo effect, the audience cheered.

Then came a FLASH! Stage lights flared, and the band was off. The keyboardist laid down swathes of sound, punctuated by some *Tron*-inspired trills. The guitarist complemented the mix with a sustained Sus2 chord played through several layers of chorus pedals and bathed in reverb. Through the murk, she managed to wring out tones like they were coming from a Trident submarine trapped in the Mariana Trench.

Then Rory, wearing a puffy spacesuit, flew down from the rafters on a rope like John Wilkes Booth after shooting Lincoln. Once onstage, he bounced around looking like Ziggy Stardust playing the Michelin Man.

By now, everyone, even the industry heavyweights and junk-bond brokers in the VIP seats, had gotten to their feet.

Rory's set began with a song from his last album, *Where Were You When They Dropped the Big One?* It was about his imagined death onstage in a nuclear holocaust. His throaty baritone filled the house, and the audience roared as he sang a local shoutout, "If they had lived/What would they say/That it was smoggiest they'd seen in L.A.?"

Then Rory & Co. went straight into *The Monster in My Pants*, a dark tune involving sex, drugs, and self-abuse in North London, played to a happy beat. The song ended, and

Rory zipped backstage. After a short break, presumably for more blow, he returned to his adoring audience waving his ivory-colored keytar. It was the most awesome mobile keyboard that anyone watching had ever seen.

Maddie thought about her fellow Raddies at home. What they wouldn't give to be here now, watching in the flesh, and not on some grainy bootleg YouTube video.

Rory pulled out some New Wave wraparound shades and led the band into *Mind Fazer.* With tongue-in-cheek, stripped-down earnestness, he screamed, "She was a mind fazer/a space chaser/a lip-tripper/one and two and three and..." Rory's nimble fingers cascaded around the keytar while he bent notes and wobbled them around like "go get 'em" chase scenes in *Miami Vice.*

When the song ended and the applause died down, Rory chucked the shades into the audience. The audience tore into them like sharks in a frenzy. Then he launched into a couple more numbers that Maddie didn't recognize. Her fingers twitched in frustration at not being able to Shazam the songs.

He introduced the next song as "an old chestnut written by a dear friend." It was a slowed-down and stripped-down version of Wang Chung's *Dance Hall Days,* delivered in a sinister sneer that made the already disturbing lines about taking your baby by the ear and playing upon her darkest fears even more chilling. Still… its scary vibe was somewhat negated by his hilariously puffy spacesuit.

Maddie wiped a tear, as the song had made her contemplate her mortality for the first time. And without her smartphone, she was left to ponder her place in the universe and the ultimate futility of life. She turned to look at Monroe, thinking with a twinge of melancholy about her time with him and the love affair that was not to be. If only she could suck down those thoughts by checking her Instagram feed.

Before all hope was lost, Rory and his band sprang to back raucous life, playing *Factory*, a punked-out number with a repetitive chorus—"I'll press a button to the boss!"—and everyone around slamdanced with abandon.

An inebriated guy with an upturned collar and a Captain Kirk-like sense of importance pogoed up to Maddie and pinched her.

"What the fuck?!" she demanded.

He looked at her, cross-eyed. His last words before passing out and hitting the ground were, "But I'm Huey Lewis!"

"More like Huey Loser," snapped Maddie, who turned to a sea of disapproving faces around her. She suddenly realized that he and his bad News band were still revered. His great downfall with *The Power of Love* and *American Psycho* wouldn't have happened yet. *Oh well*, she shrugged. *At least I wasn't molested by Phil Collins.*

The band rocked through a few more numbers as Rory and his magic keytar bounced around the stage. After a while, though, he started to sputter like an unwinding toy mouse. He was losing his breath, leaving the bass player, a brunette who donned a silver spacesuit bikini, to sing all the choruses by herself.

The medley ended, the crowd roared, and Rory took a bow.

Then he fell over.

*Oh, noooooooooo!* she thought. *What if Rory passes out for good? What if he has to go the hospital or—Jesus, no—dies?* Maddie was struck with terror at the thought of never being able to get back to the 21st century. Sure, there were pandemics, and TikTok in the future, but nothing as stupid and senseless as this fucking 1983.

Maddie turned to Monroe and Jaia. "I hate to leave you guys in the '80s without a proper goodbye, but I've got to get to Rory before it's too late."

She hugged the two of them, then gave Monroe a heartfelt kiss. "I'm going to miss you," she told him. "I hope you know that."

"Me too, Maddie. Me too."

Jaia warmly waved her goodbye.

Maddie pushed through the crowd and was about to climb up on the stage riser when she was seized by Rory's manager.

"Where the fuck do you think you're going?" Sid demanded.

Rory, still on his back with his keytar, caught sight of the drama. "It's okay, Sid. Bring her backstage."

Rory signaled to the band to commence jamming while roadies ran over to lift him to his feet. The audience cheered when he gave them the thumbs-up sign. The keyboard player stood up, donned an overcoat and Ray-Bans, then pulled a Fedora over her lush mane. She grabbed an alto sax and jammed on chorus after chorus with a vibrato sure to appease all the fans of beer commercials.

The music was still going when Rory came limping backstage to see Maddie. He smiled weakly, only showing one or two rotting teeth.

"Weedham, where do you think you're going?" Sid demanded. "The crowd wants more!"

Rory's face was flush; he did not look well. "Look, Sid. You're gonna have to go out there and tell 'em I fell ill."

Sid left in a huff, mumbling something to the effect that Rory couldn't hold a candle to his "more professional" brother, Rhys.

Rory motioned for Maddie to follow him through the dressing room and into the quickie closet.

She balked. "Listen, I'm not going to fuck you again. We had a deal."

He reached up to what looked like a large ventilation duct and unscrewed its cover. A ladder came down. "Get over yourself," he told her. He signaled for her to climb it. "Ladies first."

With trepidation but also determination, she did. When she reached the ladder's final rung, a swirl of wind sucked her up into a dark vortex. Rory must've followed, for she could hear him groan and fart as they both made their bumpy ascension.

Finally, they both ended up back where they started: in the basement of Rory's house. Now dressed back in 2020s garb, he stumbled back to his Eames chair. He reached under it and whipped out a bottle of Guinness. He offered her one, saying he was sorry but they'd drunk through all the Newcastle.

She declined. It had been a long, scary, adventure-filled weekend, and she was beat. She just wanted to go back to her place and mellow, maybe binge-watch something on Hulu.

As she turned to leave, Rory returned her iPhone. She was surprised that she'd almost forgotten about it. Then, the keytarman held up Monroe's retro-faked phone and told her that she might as well take it. She took it and held it close, deciding to keep it as a reminder of her brief but beautiful time with Monroe and their shared adventure.

Rory didn't bother walking her to the door, but Maddie didn't mind. She just needed some time to herself.

As she walked through Monroe's old neighborhood, the area looked a lot better to her. It was sketchy, but still—there were no crack dens, S&M bungalows, or Reagan Youth. *Jeez, who knew the 1980s was as bad as it was?* Were all the old-timers who'd told her how great it had been then just looking at the world through coke-covered glasses? Or, like Uncle Rico in *Napoleon Dynamite*, just trying to relive some imagined glory days?

She got to the bus stop and sat down on the bench. A Tesla sped by, blasting *Smells Like Teen Spirit* through its open windows.

That gave her an idea. *Nirvana and 'net surfing, Monica Lewinsky, and Megabyte Mondays?!* That sounded okay to her. If she was going to go retro again, at least in the 1990s they eventually got the internet and cell phones. Sure, there was the legally proscribed "Must See TV" on NBC, but she could take a little *Frasier* so long as there was *Seinfeld.* And if you were drunk enough *and* not paying attention, *Dawson's Creek* and *Melrose Place* weren't really *that* bad.

The bus arrived, its air shocks noisily welcoming her aboard. Maddie hopped on. She took a seat and pulled her phone from her back pocket. It still had a charge. She went to her Etsy app. She favorited several vintage croptops and drain-pipe jeans, then she cranked The Spice Girls and did some swiping in search of a guy who was into grunge.

# The Boys of Bummer
Staci Layne Wilson

"Look," I snap, drawing myself up to my full 6' 3" height—and with my beret, I'm an inch taller, "you two have a choice. Agree to one more concert, or stand trial. It's very simple. Choose the former, you get to serve your country; choose the latter, there's a good chance you could get the chair."

As the principal military advisor to the President, Secretary of Defense, and National Security Council, I, General Mark M. Mills, am aware that I cut an imposing figure. The scrawny knuckleheads seated across the interrogation room table from me sure are shaking in their spandex.

The alleged lead singer, David Snell, is a real piece of work—he insists that people call him Vid rather than Dave, and I'm told his vocal register falls somewhere between a rusty pump and fingernails on a chalkboard. The sorry excuse for a guitarist, Roland Par, ain't much of a prize, either—he claims he can play his instrument via mental telepathy but chooses to use his hands so he won't make Eddie Van Halen jealous. His guitar sits propped against the cinderblock wall behind his chair; it looks like something he picked up in a pawnshop for $10.

These dinky-dicks call their duo The DINKS, which stands for "double income, no kids." I believe them on the no kids thing, but I did my research and I know they haven't earned a red cent for their music. So if they take my deal, not only will they save their pencil-necks, they'll get a nice, big check from Uncle Sam.

"But we didn't do anything wrong," Vid stammers. "We were just giving a free concert in the park."

"Yeah. Since when is that a crime?" whines Roland, holding up his shackles and rattling them. Like that's supposed to make me feel sorry for him. What a sniveler.

Allow me to give you a visual of these pantywaists: Vid's neon pink shirt is three sizes too big, his parachute pants are an insult to humanity, on his girly little feet are bright green Crocs, and he's got long, greasy Jheri curls that would last about two milliseconds under my command. Roland is wearing an orange jumpsuit (not prison-issue; he actually chose to wear that onstage), hippy-dippy Birkenstock sandals, and his hair is shellacked into a fauxhawk with so much spray, he's a serious fire hazard. Did he learn nothing from that fairy, Michael Jackson?

I'd just as soon throw these two in the clink for mass murder, but believe it or not, they could be useful to the U.S. military. Hard to swallow, I know, but I'll explain.

You see, we've got troops in Panama right now, enforcing Operation Nifty Package. That bastard dictator Manuel Noriega is still holed up at the embassy, and we aren't allowed to go in with guns blazing. So, we've been going in with music blasting. We've got that shit on loudspeakers at deafening volumes, going around the clock. But even K.C. and the Sunshine Band, Alice Cooper, and Black Sabbath haven't smoked that oxygen thief out yet.

When my brother, Sheriff Joe Bob (that's him guarding the door), called to tell me about these two, I couldn't believe my ears. But I must admit, I am desperate, and his idea is pretty damn good. Vid and Roland haven't been formally charged yet, but a lot of people are dead thanks to them, and I'm just trying to make this into a win/win.

"No, it is not a crime to give a free concert in the park," I agreed. "But you've got a real soup sandwich on your hands when your entire audience commits suicide on the spot."

Or a solution. When my brother told me that he had the answer to our Noriega problem sitting in his interrogation room, I hopped a military jet lickety-split. Not only can we use these FREDs (for you civilians, that's Fucking Retards, Extra Dumb) to clear out bunkers, but their music can convince the lib-tards their pathetic lives aren't worth living, and who knows? Maybe we can even send the DINKS' so-called songs out into space via satellite to prevent any of those little green gooks from invading our planet.

I angle myself just so, ensuring that the fluorescent light bar hanging from the ceiling reflects off my chest candy. I cross my arms and give them my best Stonewall Jackson glare. "So... what'll it be, boys?"

...

I start humming, and Roland wills his guitar to play. The sheriff and the general look at us with confused expressions, but then, too late—they understand what's happening. Mark Mills is quicker on the draw, grabbing Joe Bob's sidearm from its holster. He brings the .357 Magnum to his temple. BLAM! The gun clatters to the ground, and the sheriff picks it up and brings the muzzle to his chin. He fights the urge longer than most, but the end result is the same: our band is "No. 1 with a bullet."

## Bite It Out
Brenda Thatcher

Worn pickup trucks and dirty sedans fill the parking lot in front of Cherrie's Bar and Diner. Despite the various makes and models, they each bear a striking resemblance. The now-dried mud splashes across the fenders and the rain-dampened dirt that clouds the paint. Some of the trucks carry rifle racks in the bed, while the majority of sedans wear ski racks atop their roofs.

New arrivals to the city would think it was Community's Square Dancing night. Why not? It was Boring, Oregon, after all—and yeah, the city lived up to its name. But tonight? No. Not Square Dancing. This is Benatar Night at Cherrie's. Better—it's Halloween.

Why does that matter? The owner is a major music fan, and a couple of years ago her favorite artist, Pat Benatar, rocked the L.A. Sports Arena on Halloween night. So, since then, Cherrie's offered an homage to that artist and that event. In costume, of course.

This year, I wear plastic vampire teeth to make a game of the song *Fight It Out* from her *Get Nervous* album. Get it? The title changed to *Bite It Out*? What the hell, I'll take what I can get. Too bad the song didn't make it to MTV. It would have rocked. Her power? Her range? Yeah, I'm also a fan.

Haven't seen her since the 1982 *Precious Time* tour, and now *Wide Awake in Dreamland* is out, but I'll take what I can get. "Radical!"

The car door is sticky, so I elbow it to force its compliance. The metal screams as it opens. Rain's sultry scent wraps me. The crash of keyboards and syncopated lyrics from the bar's outside sound system identifies Falco's *Rock me, Amadeus.* Unexpected, but way better than that hellish *Heaven is a Place on Earth* by the Carlisle twit.

The car door requires two slams before it closes. The lock needs some WD-40 but it finally engages, after my obligatory muttering and cursing. The rain is a surprising waterfall, which doesn't do any favors to my teased and spritzed 'do. "Dude! Seriously?"

But, it's cool.

I tug up my coat's hood and head off.

The increasing puddles manage to turn the bottom of my jeans into soaked sponges by the time I make it to the bar's entrance.

Inside, I shuck my dripping coat, hang it on a handy peg by the doorway, then bend over from the waist to rescue my hair.

Sure, not the most graceful position, especially considering the weight I'd gained sitting in study hall at the college, but this position makes gathering my long, kinky hair into my fist far, far easier. Now, I just need… Which pocket? I always kept them handy, so…wait. The back one.

*Success!*

The hair scrunchie wrapping my wrist is a familiar and comforting caress against my skin. A pull and a few twists and *viola!* I straighten and check myself in the window's reflection. Me in a Pebble Flintstone hairstyle, torn jeans, a bulky chartreuse sweater, and I have enough bangles on my arms that I look like a roll of Lifesavers.

Satisfied and confident, I head deeper into the building. Shoulder pads galore, shades of teal and fuchsia everywhere on the dance floor, leg warmers, mullets, and more hair than anyone would think was possible. Each shellacked strand looks ready to make a desperate attempt to escape the teasing comb and Aqua Net.

Wait… aren't there supposed to be Halloween costumes? I mean, I was trying for the *Flashdance* chick. Jeez, am I the only one?

"Dude! Bummer."

The people dancing past me look happy and flushed. Drinks make the rounds on the trays held by wait staff in overly tight clothing. Some dude in the corner puts his face to the table and inhales a line of coke à la *Scarface*. No hesitation. No fear.

Awesome!

Some waiter in those too-tight jeans stops in front of me with a tray of tumblers containing dark liquid and topped by something amber. A slice of white separates the two colors, making a sort of a flag of booze. He smiles and extends the tray, saying: "On the house."

Really? Like I'm gonna say "no" to free booze.

As if.

I take one and navigate my plastic teeth to successfully sip it. Kahlua, Bailey's, and something with a hint of orange. Delight floods me, as does the alcohol's heat. Amazing. "Omigod, what is this?"

His smile widens and his gaze drops to my chest for a moment. Yeah, I'm chesty. Came into my breasts early, so that's nothing new. Neither is his pervy smirk.

"It's called a B-52. One of the bartender's favorites," he says.

"Like the airplane?"

The waiter laughs, says, "Exactly like the airplane," then vanishes into the crowd.

I am left alone and with a drink that's

melting me from the inside, the only one wearing a Halloween costume, listening to MTV's Top Hits instead of a cover band, and I don't give a whoop.

Not one single fuck.

I head to the bar and hand over my backpack and a 20-dollar bill to the amiable bartender, Eric. He's my best friend's older brother, so I can get away with asking him to watch my belongings. I mean, that's what a friend's family is for, right?

"I'm off at midnight," Eric says and tucks it beneath the bar. "Be back for this shit before it happens."

"Bummer!"

He snaps a bar towel against my fingers. "I'm serious, Megan."

I sigh an aggrieved "Fi-ine" and use my reflection in the back bar mirror to touch up my lip gloss. He tweaks my Pebbles ponytail and I blow him a kiss. The way his attention keeps returning to my visible cleavage tells me he's interested.

Too bad he's so old.

I like his truck.

With a deliberate jiggle of my chest and a toss of my hair, I head onto the dance floor. Soon enough, I am swept into the colored lights refracting off the large ball overhead, the pounding throb of music, and the moist mass of heaving humanity.

Myself one of them, bouncing and heaving

to the music. It isn't long before I have a group of girls dancing with me. As a group, we go to the bar, the bathroom, and eventually, there's just one girl at my side.

"Megan," I say while we stand in front of the bathroom mirror.

"Sam," she says, streaking her lips with my tube of Strawberry Glaze.

Her voice is low and gravelly, like she's spent too much time sucking on cigarettes. All the same, she's a super dance partner with her fluffy hair, and a fragile tutu of cream crowning neon pink leggings with electric blue leg warmers. Around her neck is a sparkling choker. Oh, and that long nose is a bonus, because I look better than she does. Not gonna lie.

I must've bit through the fake fangs earlier. They droop annoyingly, so I toss 'em in the trash. "Sam? Like Samantha on *Bewitched?*"

She puts her index finger on her nose and pushes it back and forth while saying "tinka-tinka-tinka."

So stupid and yet so, "OMG, That's so *Bewitched!* Awesome!"

We laugh and push through the bathroom doors on our way back to the dance floor. Eric is waving at me, so I change direction and head his way, Sam following along. She's cool, so no biggie. I get there and Eric slams my backpack onto the bar, nearly on my hands.

"Time to go home," he states.

"Now? But I'm having fun!"

"Megan..."

"It's not midnight yet." But it's close, or close enough. Five minutes until.

A smiling Sam moves closer. "I'll take care of her."

Eric shoots her an unfriendly look. "That wasn't our agreement."

Now Sam isn't smiling, and Eric looks a little too pleased with himself.

Those shots of booze I downed earlier give me the needed courage to take a stand. "I'm staying."

"No—"

"You can't force me."

"Yes, I can."

Eric and I engage in a staring contest, neither giving way until Sam breaks the silence.

"I know what you want," she says, low-voiced.

She gives an encouraging nod.

Eric's brows crash together like a thundercloud. "Take it easy."

I remind them both, "I'm an adult now."

Midnight arrives with a ringing of bells and a lowering of the lights. Servers exit the kitchen, each with a banquet tray on their shoulders that is laden with what looks to be a mountain of mashed potatoes. Howling people dive at the mountain, and it becomes clear that's not potatoes. Coke. On the house. For everyone

Go home now? Oh, hell no!

I head for the mob. "Just leave my backpack wherever. I'll find it before I go."

Eric's response is unsurprisingly foul. The distance between us widens, and the volume of the howling crowd increases in counterpoint to The Bangles on the sound system, but somehow I can still hear them.

"It'll be okay," Sam says, and Eric's reply is, "Counting on you."

I spin back around and hold up my middle finger, shouting, "I don't need your help!"

Sam is closer than I realized, but isn't offended by the gesture. She catches my wrist and pulls me sideways, saying, "That stuff's garbage. The good shit is over here. Come."

I follow Sam, but glance backward. Eric looks... defeated.

So he should! I'm not a child!

We go up the stairs to the second floor, to the sound of "Walk Like an Egyptian" winding down. Sam guides me to the manager's office. I hang back, but she smiles and pulls a key from inside her bra.

An always-available storage area.

Another benefit of being stacked.

We slip inside the shadowed office, and I close the door behind me. Sam, with an eager squeal, heads toward the oversized desk. She dives face-first into a mountain of white powder. The sound of greedy inhalation fills the air. *Sniffffffff.*

A gasp follows, then a giggle.

Well, like, good shit, yeah? I can wait.

I head to the wall-length window. It's just like in the movies, where the boss gazes down onto the consumers and employees below. I feel so empowered to be there, and a bit thrilled.

It's The Boss's office, and I'm in it.

Me. Wait...

I strain closer to the window, not believing my own eyes. People look to be running and falling, bleeding, and vomiting. The wait staff appears to be standing by and watching. Worse! Did that chick just knock that other chick back into the growing pile of writhing people? "What's going on?"

"I told you that wasn't the good stuff." Sam's chuckle raises the hairs on my arms. Sultry. Inappropriate. Creepy. Just as she is now, with her face smeared in white power and her hardened nipples covered with the same.

She licks her lips—her tongue is waaay too long for her mouth—then uses her index finger to paint those lips with more of the white powder. It sparkles eerily, like the scales of a fish kissed by sunlight.

Over the sound system, Benatar breaks into *Fight It Out*, the song that inspired my

Halloween costume, but I don't have time to listen. I head for the door. Sam catches me and sweeps me off my feet, and slams me down onto the wooden desk hard enough to force my breath from my lungs.

Shocked breathless, I stare at the girl I thought was friendly. Her face gets larger and larger as she presses closer and closer to mine...then presses her powdered lips to mine. A lance of fire travels from my mouth and into my brain. I squeal and kick, or try to, anyway. A strange weight pulls at my limbs, the strength leeching from my muscles.

Quaaludes? Shit! Eric tried to warn me...

Sam's busy unsnapping my jeans and yanking them from my legs. They dangle limply. My undies are torn away with a single yank. I can only manage a protesting twitch, which doesn't bother my attacker. In fact, it appears to turn her on. She flips up her tutu and yanks down her leggings.

A dick springs eagerly from Sam's crotch.

*What the fuck?*

That isn't the greatest horror by far. No, it's that the unexpected pole of meat HAS TEETH! Not the fake kind. No. Sam's phallus has five rows of diagonal, needle-like gnashers.

A shark's mouth coming for my twat!

Sam lays the length of it against my labia and rocks against my crotch. The mouth at the tip clashes its teeth, a demanding *snap-snap-snap.* I manage a mewling sound.

Sam smiles down at me. So many teeth.

She reaches and positions her second head's sharp teeth onto my clit. It bites down.

The pain is a hot, electric sizzle along my nerves. A high whine slips from my throat. I struggle to kick, to punch, to escape. Futile. Tears track my face. My body won't respond. All it does is feel...

Sliding. Surging.

The drag of those vicious teeth along each millimeter of my ruined flesh.

Sam pumps and gasps. Our bodies slap together with a desperate sound of skin thwacking skin. She hisses her ecstasy, the sound of steaks atop a hot grill. Shock drags at me, and my vision narrows and blackens.

I fall into the darkness to the sound of Benatar's exquisite, operatic voice rising to a crescendo. The words...so relevant...all about the hurt inside... all about the tears I...

We hope you enjoyed *Rock & Roll Nightmares: Gory Days*, the '80s edition. If you did, please kindly leave a review, and be on the lookout for the other books in this series.

## Author Bios

**Staci Layne Wilson** is an L.A. native who enjoys traffic, wildfires, and earthquakes—but since her recent move to Las Vegas, she's learned to love 110-degree summers, drive-thru wedding chapels, and casinos that still reek of the Rat Pack's cigars. The best day of Staci's life was when she got to interview Jack White and Jimmy Page on the red carpet for *It Might Get Loud*. She has directed a music documentary— *The Ventures: Stars on Guitars*, about her dad's band—and her next film, cowritten with Darren Gordon Smith, is *The Second Age of Aquarius*, a sci-fi rock & roll rom-com. Catch up with Staci at www.stacilaynewilson.com

**Mark Wheaton** is a novelist (*The Quake Cities*, *Emily Eternal*) and screenwriter (*Friday the 13th*, *The Messengers*) originally from Texas. One of the craziest shows he ever saw was a Butthole Surfers' New Year's Eve show in Houston in his teen years. There was fire, rioting, a blackout, and the next time he hit that club—the late, great Vatican—a heavy wooden barrier had been constructed in front of the stage, the bouncers shrugging when he asked what it was for saying, "Damn Surfers show." Follow Wheaton's typing at https://www.facebook.com/MarkWheaton42/

**Darren Gordon Smith** is a filmmaker, writer, and musician. He is the co-creator of *Repo! The Genetic Opera*, which is considered by *Rolling Stone* magazine to be one of the top 25 cult films of all time and stars Anthony Head, Sarah Brightman, and Ogre of Skinny Puppy. Darren plays a mean keytar.

**Sean McDonough** keeps the '80s style alive with his catalog of gleefully gruesome horror novels, all available now on Amazon. His latest book, *The Thirteen Black Cats of Edith Penn*, will be out Fall 2021. His first real concert was Killswitch Engage and In Flames at the Hammerstein Ballroom, and that's the only biographical aspect of this story, please and thank you. Get all of Sean's latest news on Instagram @HouseoftheBoogeyman

**Violet Castro** is a Mexican American writer originally from Texas now residing in the UK. She is the author of *Hairspray and Switchblades*, *Goddess of Filth* and *The Queen of The Cicadas*. Violet's dream concerts would be Iron Maiden, Lita Ford, and Metallica. Her favorite couple in music is June Carter and Johnny Cash. You can follow her on Twitter and Instagram @vlatinalondon

**Brenda Thatcher** is an author and screenwriter who loves Pat Benatar's *Shadows of the Night* and thinks that Toni Basil's song *Mickey* is the worst earworm of all time. Upcoming projects include a short film of her story *The White Mare* to be produced by Ghost Walk Studios, and she is also busy pitching her first sci-fi/action feature screenplay, *Starfire*.

## Audiobook Narrator Bio

**Andy Garrison** has been a professional actor since 1985, when he was listening to bands like The Rainmakers, Dire Straits, and those purveyors of swamp-a-delic funk-a-billy, Webb Wilder and the Beatnecks. He teaches acting, commercial voiceover and audiobook narration at his acting studio, ATS—the Actor Training Studio. Andy and his wife Allise enjoy the vibrant arts scene and diversity that come with living—and eating—in Kansas City, home of the 3 B's: Blues, Beer and Barbecue. Catch up with Andy at actortrainingstudio.com

**Special thanks**—Aaron Kai, Lotti Pharriss-Knowles, Alex Burton, Rob Acocella, Sonya Bateman, Sadie Hartmann (aka, "Mother Horror"), and last but far from least, Linda Rose.